ECB

THE HOUSE ON
HOLLY STREET

THE HOUSE ON HOLLY STREET

•

Mary Catherine Hanson

AVALON BOOKS
NEW YORK

PRINTED IN THE UNITED STATES OF AMERICA
ON ACID-FREE PAPER
BY HADDON CRAFTSMEN, BLOOMSBURG, PENNSYLVANIA

To my grandson Christian Hanson
and his brothers Ronnie, Freddie, and Falesima.

Chapter One

Francesca Mayhew gazed out at the soft gray landscape of Edgecombe from behind the dingy glass window of an old taxicab. She was deep in thought, and watched the passing scenery without much interest. She did not distinguish the mingling church steeples and magnificent old houses surrounded by broad green lawns that swept down to immaculate white fences. Through the spaces separating the houses she glimpsed the colorless bay, rimmed by frothy white foam splashing onto the shore, and the white sails of a few boats skimming over the sunless water.

Edgecombe, Connecticut, was a town as near to perfection as any place on earth could possibly be. It had been carefully planned and laid out by the founders, who had been shipowners and sea captains. They had sailed on perilous voyages, trading with the Far East and the West Indies, making enormous fortunes and bringing home untold treasures.

1

They left an indelible mark of elegance, and a tradition of pride to be upheld by descendants.

I'm home, Francesca thought. *I'm at my mother's home*. She gave a mental shrug. Having been the daughter of a career diplomat, she had never really lived any place long enough to call home. Home was called ''post'' in diplomatic circles.

Autumn, in its most brilliant dress of red and gold hues scattering dead leaves onto the ground and making beautiful abstract patterns on the green grass failed to rouse Francesca from her despondency. Her hands lay on her lap so tightly clasped, one could imagine the blood flowing away from her knuckles. She suddenly felt the labored effort that the old car made as it changed gears to make its trek up the hill to Holly Street. They passed the old town cemetery where many of Edgecombe's founders rested. The Englishes, the Todds, the Lynches, and the Gaylords.

Well, one Gaylord will not rest here. She sighed, and closed her eyes for a brief moment, only catching a glimpse of gray weathered headstones, where green lichen and time were slowly erasing the names of the founders.

Was it only a week ago, she thought as she breathed in deeply, that friends from the embassy had rushed to the small school where she taught, to tell her that there had been an accident, and she had to go to the hospital immediately? They did not tell her that it was already too late.

Her father had been posted for two years in this small African country. That day he had been on his way to an unimportant luncheon with her mother.

The small red, white, and blue flags of the United States were flying from each fender announcing that the Ambassador was in the car. No note was taken of this as two warring factions fired on each other, catching her parents and their driver in the crossfire, killing them instantly. There had been a flurry of investigations, but no one was apprehended, and, doubtless, never would be.

After the brief funeral ceremony at Arlington Cemetery, which she had gone through in a trance, her mother's aunts had persuaded her to come to their home in Edgecombe, and now she was almost there.

The taxi crawled to a stop. The driver peered through the rearview mirror at Francesca, who had made no effort to get out of the car.

"This is it, Miss," he said.

"Oh! Thank you." She hurriedly opened the door. She walked up to an old iron gate. Brown rust was beginning to show through the black paint. Her eyes were fixed on the old Victorian house whose grandeur seemed to be on a downward path.

"Miss!" She heard the driver call. She looked back at him and he pointed to the gate with his chin, urging her through. She followed his directions and lifted the latch, which felt like ice. She opened the gate and walked slowly up the brick path to the house that sat on a rise.

She twisted the old-fashioned doorbell that turned like a key. She heard it ring on the other side of the door, then the soft tread of slow-moving footsteps coming toward the door.

"Yes?" The door was opened by Ruth, an old employee.

"I'm Francesca." She was saved any more effort in trying to jog Ruth's memory when a tall, stately woman appeared at the door, her silver hair superbly coiled in a French twist and tied back with a black lace band. She pulled the door open wider.

"Oh, my goodness, it's Francesca." The woman, Lelia, exclaimed.

Daisy was halfway down the stairs when she heard Francesca's name. She ignored the bulk of her body and bounded down the rest of the steps, calling Francesca's name.

The two sisters greeted their niece with love and a heartfelt compassion. Daisy held Francesca's hands at arm's length, carefully studying her to see how much of a toll this young woman had paid in her grief. For a moment they both remembered the little girl with the long dark hair, and the most beautiful brown eyes heavily fringed with thick dark lashes. Now she stood before them, a very elegant young woman with a certain light of youth forever extinguished from her eyes.

She was dressed in a brown tweed chesterfield coat, elegance shining through the understatement of her clothes. Her luxuriant hair was now cut to her shoulders. It flipped up slightly at the ends and was caught on each side with mock-tortoiseshell combs framing a perfect oval face the color of honey and apricot. Her cheeks glowed pink from the cold, and her full coral lips were damp from nervousness; but this disadvantage did not disturb the presence that she bore.

The aunts looked upon her with great pride. Even with the name Mayhew, Francesca was indeed Gaylord blood.

Francesca's eyes adjusted to the dim light in the entrance hall, and in a brief survey of her surroundings, she saw a faded red silk damask wall covering. There were two unlighted brass sconces on either side of the pocket doors that once had been gaslit.

Francesca's eyes wandered up the oak staircase and came to rest on a young woman standing in the shadows observing her shyly. When their eyes met, she descended the steps with her hand outstretched.

"Hello, Francesca. I'm Amelia. Do you remember me?"

Francesca studied the young woman's face for a moment before the dark haunting eyes touched her memory. Her thoughts flashed back to the little girl who had suddenly appeared at her aunts' house and who seemed so lost and out of place. Francesca remembered her strange behavior one snowy morning at breakfast. For no reason, Amelia had picked up her cereal bowl and peered under it, then did the same thing with the sugar dish. Aunt Lelia had asked, "What are you looking for, Amelia?" With sad eyes, the little girl had shrugged thin shoulders and answered, "Something that belongs to me." No one ever discovered what that something was and Aunt Lelia had said kindly, "Eat your cereal, Amelia."

"Of course I do," Francesca said, embracing

Amelia "There's just more to both of us now." And the two young women laughed together.

"Where is your luggage, Francesca?" Lelia thought to ask.

"Oh, my goodness," Francesca exclaimed as a loud thud sounded at the door and she hastened to answer it.

"I forgot all about the taxi driver." She opened the door and found the taxi driver standing, loaded down with suitcases and not a free hand to ring the bell, so he had used a foot. Looking somewhat put out, the driver asked in a voice filled with vexation, "Miss, where do you want these bags?"

Lelia took command and with a wave of her long bony hand toward the stairs, ordered the driver without any qualms, "Please take the luggage up to Miss Mayhew's room. As you can see, we are short on help here."

The driver gave Lelia a look of bewilderment and rolled his eyes to the heavens. As far as he was concerned, his obligation ended at the front door, but under such a stern command, he decided not to argue the point and did as the old lady bade him do.

"Go with him, Ruth," she added. So without another word, the taxi driver followed Ruth up the stairs, bumping luggage against the walls as he trudged up the steps.

"Come in, child, and sit by the fire. You must be cold." Daisy gently steered Francesca to the sitting room where a quiet fire burned in a white marble fireplace. Ornate Victorian furniture upholstered in dark red velvet crowded the room. Francesca warmed her hands before the fire and gazed into the yellow dancing flames that flickered across her face. Without warning, an overwhelming sense of loneliness surged over her, and tears welled in her eyes and spilled down her cheeks as her body trembled with soft sobbing.

"Oh, my dear, there, there," Daisy said, cradling Francesca in her large arms. "I know it's not easy, but always remember we love you and want you here with us. It seems that families are linked together by a chain of sadness, and all we can do is hold on as tightly as we can, becoming stronger as we go." She stroked Francesca's hair gently. "After a while the pain eases and we slowly start to remember the good times. You will see, my dear."

Lelia stood back with her hands folded before her. Even though she shared the same ache and compassion for Francesca, she could not show her emotions as Daisy so lovingly did, so she simply observed the tender scene with a haughty look down her aquiline nose, but for a second her thin lips trembled.

The uneasy moment was quelled by the appearance of Amelia bearing a beautiful silver tea service. Francesca withdrew from Daisy's arms and dried her eyes. Amelia pretended not to notice that Francesca had been crying and busied herself, finding the right spot to place the tray on the mahogany table before the fireplace.

"There," she said cheerfully as she surveyed the setting.

"Let's all have some hot tea and then you can get the travel dirt off and rest for a spell before lunch,"

Lelia said, taking the helm again. With an afterthought she added, ''Perhaps Amelia will help you unpack later.''

''Oh, I'd love to.'' Amelia smiled at Francesca.

''Thank you, Amelia.'' She smiled back at the young woman whose searching eyes sparkled with new expectation.

Francesca was already beginning to feel better. The hot tea had soothed her nerves and she was ready to rest after the long and heartbreaking journey of returning home with the bodies of her parents and the quick burial services in Arlington Cemetery with Washington dignitaries.

So to the faint sound of damp winds rustling dried autumn leaves, Francesca fell into a sound sleep and did not stir until early evening. Darkness had settled in the room and she awakened to the yellow glow of a fire crackling in the grate that made dancing shadows of immobile objects on the walls. Francesca contemplated the room in the faint light of the fire. The room was papered in a dark rose damask and her bed was the most beautiful brass bed that she had ever seen in her life. It had four posts that were carved with the design of a rope with grape leaves twining up to the top where a damask canopy spread out over the bed, draping down into heavy folds of fabric, giving Francesca the cozy feeling of shutting out the world.

At the sound of the door creaking, Francesca turned to see Amelia's head peek around the corner as she planned to gently awaken Francesca. She tiptoed through the door and called softly, "Francesca, are you awake?"

Francesca raised up on her elbows, smiled at Amelia's gentle intrusion, and said, "Yes, I'm awake, Amelia."

"My, you slept away the whole afternoon. Aunt Lelia said that we had better awaken you for dinner. It's almost ready." Amelia switched on the overhead light and went to the luggage still sitting on the floor where the taxi driver had left it.

"What would you like to wear?" Amelia asked, swinging the suitcase onto a nearby chair.

"I guess any skirt and sweater," Francesca said, getting out of bed.

Francesca and Amelia unpacked the suitcases, with Amelia practically swooning over some of the clothes Francesca had bought in cities all over the world in her travels with her parents.

"Oh, Francesca, how beautiful," Amelia exclaimed, holding up a luxurious daffodil-yellow angora sweater before her; she turned and twisted glamorously before the mirror, the brilliant yellow illuminating her dark hair.

"You can have it." Francesca grinned admiringly at Amelia.

"Oh, no, Francesca," Amelia protested weakly.

"It looks much too pretty on you. So I insist without another word." Francesca waved aside any more words of protest from Amelia, who at once removed her sweater and put her new one on. Running to the mirror again, she caressed the soft sweater, letting the fluffy hairs run through her fingers.

"It is so beautiful. Thank you so much, Francesca."

"You're most welcome. I'm ready to go downstairs now."

"Good. I'm going to wear my sweater to show Aunt Lelia and Aunt Daisy."

The dining room was pleasantly decorated with a yellow silk moiré wall covering that had faded with the years but nevertheless glowed cheerfully in the light of the translucent fluted globes of the brass chandelier. Lelia sat at the head of the table in her finest black dress. A delicate crescent brooch of sparkling diamonds and pearls caught the light of the chandelier and sent tiny flashes of light from her throat. Daisy sat at the other end of the table. She too wore her finest silk dress, but it was not the austere black of Lelia's; it was a cheerful blue with creamy white roses scattered through it.

"What a lovely sweater," Daisy said, noticing Amelia's new sweater.

"Francesca gave it to me." Amelia beamed, enfolding herself into her arms. "Isn't it beautiful?"

"Lovely, dear." Lelia nodded her head in approval.

Dinner was simple, but tasty. Ruth, with the help of Lelia, Daisy, and Amelia, had baked a marvelous roast beef with baked potatoes, asparagus, and a dish of vanilla ice cream for dessert.

When dinner was finished, Ruth brought in a decanter of sherry with beautiful hand-cut crystal glasses. When each had been poured a glass of the golden liquid, Lelia raised her glass in the direction of Francesca and said, ''Welcome home, my dear.''

Daisy and Amelia raised their glasses to Francesca, whose eyes glistened brightly. She whispered softly, ''Thank you, oh, thank you for making me feel so welcome.''

Chapter Two

A few days later the sun waged a battle with the cooling winds of approaching winter and burned so furiously into the chilly morning air that by noontime Indian summer had arrived and everyone was back in shirtsleeves again and enjoying a capricious interlude.

Amelia bounded into the breakfast room where Francesca was having a quiet morning cup of coffee.

"I don't have any clients today who want to buy a house from me, so why don't we take advantage of this last fling of summer and go down to the beach?"

"What a marvelous idea. I'd like that." Francesca hurried and finished her coffee. "Should we take our bathing suits?"

"Well, the water might be a little chilly now, but let's wear them just in case it's warm enough," Amelia said.

At the beach, with dirndl skirts blowing about

their well-shaped legs, Francesca and Amelia each tested the water with a toe.

"Ooh, no." Francesca laughed, pulling her foot quickly back from the cold water. "The sun hasn't fooled the bay; it definitely says that summer is over." They laughed and spread a blanket out over the sand.

Francesca leaned back on her elbows and raised her face toward the sun.

"It's a beautiful day. I'm so glad we came." Amelia lay back and closed her eyes against the bright rays of the sun. "We won't have many more, so let's savor this one as much as we can." She inhaled deeply. "This will have to last us for a while."

Francesca played thoughtfully with the sand, letting it run slowly through her fingers as she gazed out over the bay and listened to the quiet sounds of Edgecombe going about its daily business, and she wondered how she would adjust to her new life. A sad, puzzled look filled her chestnut eyes. She did not really know Edgecombe; most of her life had been spent in far-off exotic lands filled with sophisticated people from the diplomatic service, and people of the world in general. She knew nothing of the quiet, complacent town of people who had found a niche on earth and who were content never to venture very far from home.

Will I ever fit in? Will I ever fit in anywhere? she almost said out loud, suddenly clutching the sand tightly in her fist.

As if telepathically, Amelia spoke to her through closed eyes.

"What did you do in that little country?"

"I taught school. The young children of diplomats and some of the native children."

"Did you like it?"

"Yes, once you got used to wiping runny noses and catching their colds." Francesca smiled at the memory of her young students. "The children were really very sweet, and there's a certain satisfaction in seeing their unbridled enthusiasm. They wanted to get into everything."

"What do you want to do in Edgecombe?" Amelia asked.

"I don't know. In fact, I was just thinking about that this very moment," Francesca answered.

"I have an idea," Amelia stated, opening her eyes in a squint.

"Really, what?" Francesca sounded interested.

"Well, Florence Evans is leaving our office soon to have her baby. Do you know anything about real estate?" Amelia asked.

"Nothing at all." Francesca gave a doubtful shake of her head.

"There's nothing hard about it, and you can take a course over in Eton, but in the meantime you can read up on some of the laws of real estate. People are beginning to discover our little town and are buying houses like crazy. We hope not too many, though. We don't want to become a thriving metropolis again." Amelia looked pleased, then a second thought occurred to her.

"You do drive, don't you?"

"Oh, yes," Francesca replied. "But I'll have to get a Connecticut license."

"Good. I'll take you to meet Mr. Benson tomorrow. Benson Real Estate is a nice place to work. You'll fit right in. There's Randy and Sally and, well, this guy, Bill Adams. . . . But enough about work." Amelia snuggled down again and grinned. "We won't let anything interfere with this last day of summer."

"Absolutely not," Francesca agreed, and thought for a moment. "Do you know, Amelia, I think I'm going to like this."

"I'm sure Mr. Benson is going to like you." Amelia fell silent again and closed her eyes.

Francesca continued to gaze out over the bay. Her wandering eyes came to rest on a sailboat swaying gracefully at anchor in a small cove, its rigging bare against the blue sky. "Whose magnificent boat is that?" she asked, disturbing Amelia's repose.

Amelia sat up and a look of sadness clouded her dark eyes. "That's the *Sea Song*. She belonged to Keal English." She turned to Francesca. "You must have met him at some time."

Amelia's gaze became a fixed stare as she looked at the *Sea Song*. "Keal took her out alone one day some months ago, and no one has seen him since. They found her drifting about three miles offshore. They surmise that he had accidentally fallen overboard." Amelia shrugged her slight shoulders. "And that's that."

"How awful," Francesca said.

"Yes, the Englishes and the Lynches have had a hard time, I'm afraid. Not to mention Aunt Leila and Aunt Daisy. They were very close to Keal's aunt, Isabel Lynche. They were like sisters. Lelia, Daisy, Isabel, and Charlotte. Four peas in a pod." Amelia smiled and then sadness erased the smile.

"Poor Isabel died some years ago. She never recovered from her daughter Clarissa's death in an automobile accident. She gave up and never left her room again. I use to visit her a lot with Aunt Lelia and Aunt Daisy." Amelia smiled as she remembered Isabel. "She always wore French perfume. Funny, how happiness ends," Amelia mused. "Lyre Hall, the Lynche home, is a replica of Belle Rose, the English house, and was built as a wedding present to Isabel. It's a lovely house."

Francesca thought for a moment and replied, "Life is certainly very strange." She felt the sudden chill in the wind that had become brisk, with the frail yellow sun casting lengthening shadows across the sand in its journey to the west. "Shall we leave?" she said, gathering up her beach blanket.

"Yes," Amelia answered almost in a whisper. Somehow the first joy of the day had, without warning, ebbed away and left them both deep in their own thoughts.

The two young women sauntered aimlessly back home by way of town, with Amelia reintroducing Francesca to things that had once been familiar.

"Do you remember this?" Amelia laughed, pointing to the old Revolutionary War cannon that sat on the grassy mall of the commons, turning green with age, sitting proudly with its harmless cannonballs piled in a pyramid beside it.

"Ha! Do I. . . . it was a definite disruption of a good relationship between mother and daughter. I always climbed on it, and always fell off." A forlorn look reflected in Francesca's eyes. How safe she had been, how protected. A shudder went through her body. Her placid world had been washed away forever in a matter of moments, and for the first time, she was filled with hatred. She walked away from the cannon without another word, and Amelia understood.

After dinner, which was mostly leftovers from the last night's meal, Francesca made a mental note to go grocery shopping the next day with Amelia. She would certainly help with the expense of running the house. She would never be a burden to her aunts. Her parents had been very farsighted and had left her, if not a lot of money, enough so that she would never starve to death.

Each involved themselves in their private moments of the day. Daisy went to her room to read poetry and Lelia read a novel while Amelia prepared for work the next day by washing her hair, which, in her words, "was going to take forever to dry."

This left Francesca alone with her thoughts which were still, from time to time, troublesome and making her uneasy. She sat before the fire on the red velvet Victorian sofa that was beginning to wear. She stretched her long legs out and watched the yellow flames that intermittently shot out a blue spark. The crackle of the burning log seemed to be the only sound in the house. Outside the winds were rising and she could hear the soft spattering of rain starting to fall. Francesca could feel the shadows closing in on her, bringing into focus too many memories that had not, as Daisy had promised, yet melted into the remembrance of only the good times. Pain still lurked, threatening to bring despair upon her. Francesca did not know how not to give in, but somehow she knew that she must not. She got up quickly and went to the hall closet where she quietly put on her raincoat and a pair of boots. Taking an umbrella from the wrought-iron stand nearby, she softly opened the door and stepped out into the wet night.

It was only a slight drizzle as Francesca walked down the hill toward the town. The wet, cold air had a revitalizing effect on her and was slowly blowing away the dusty cobwebs that were cluttering her mind. In the distance she saw the yellow light spreading across the sidewalk from Slocum's Stationery Store and she knew where she was going— to get the latest fashion magazines. She thought that would cheer her up, even though there would hardly be anything in them that she could afford.

''Hello, Francesca. Nice to see you again. What in the world are you doing out in this weather?'' Mr. Slocum greeted her with a cheerful grin.

''Hello, Mr. Slocum. I thought I would get some magazines before it really started to rain,'' she replied.

''Well, I've got almost everything, even got some French *Vogues* and *Bazaars*. So just help yourself.''

''Thank you.'' Francesca busied herself, thumbing

through many of the magazines before she made a choice. She took her selections to the counter where Mr. Slocum was waiting for her.

"I think I'll take these." Francesca handed the magazines across the counter to him.

"Let me see what you've got here." He peered at the magazines through his rimless half glasses. "Hmmm, two French and three U.S." He rang the sales up. "I'll put these in a bag for you. It's beginning to blow out there." Mr. Slocum walked Francesca to the door and gave her a bit of concerned advice. "You hurry on home now."

"I will. Good night, Mr. Slocum."

"Good night, Francesca." He shook his head as he shut the door and began turning out the lights; it was time for him to go home, too.

Francesca started up the hill with the rising winds pulling at her umbrella and tossing her hair wildly in every direction. She was beginning to agree with Mr. Slocum. What in the world was she doing out in weather like this? The gentle rainfall that she had first come out in had turned into a tempest with forceful winds that sent her off her path as she fought to keep her umbrella aloft while trying to protect her magazines.

The wind lifted the umbrella, clearing her vision for a brief moment. Ahead of her she saw the solitary figure of a man walking toward her, before the wind, just as suddenly as it had lifted the umbrella, dropped it again. Francesca gripped the magazines under her arm and clutched a corner of the silk canopy with her free hand. But as she did so, a rogue wind swooped down and snapped the umbrella inside out, dragging poor Francesca behind it and straight into the path of the passing pedestrian, thrusting itself into the face of the man. An oath of pain ejected from the stranger.

Francesca apologized effusively. She saw the man holding his eye and she tried to look at the injury, but he pushed her helping hand away and said gruffly, "It's all right."

She could not see his face even though a streak of lightning lit the sky for a brief second. With his hand covering his eye, Francesca saw rain-soaked hair that might have been any color clinging to his head. The lightning faded away and he removed his hand from his face, which was again in darkness.

"I am so sorry. Is there anything I can do?" she asked.

Another burst of lightning showed the back of his head as he turned from her and said in an unfriendly tone, "Aren't you somewhat ill-advised to be out on a night like this?" With these few words he walked away.

Francesca stood bewildered by the rudeness of the man, anger mounting in her. She started to call out to him that she had apologized. What more was there for her to do, and she thought, with a mischievous grin, *Aren't* you *the one who is ill-advised to be out on a night like this? After all, you're the one who got punched with the umbrella.*

She felt better after this mental attack on the stranger and she looked back once to see how he was faring when she saw the tall shadow of another man join the injured stranger from a secluded place. They spoke briefly, the man fell in step, and they walked down the hill toward town.

They seemed so secretive, Francesca thought, as she continued her climb up the hill to Holly Street with her protected magazines and her umbrella, now in shambles, dragging along beside her. She wondered, with each difficult step, why had she come out in this frightful weather.

Amelia was standing on the stairs when a dripping-wet Francesca let herself in noiselessly at the front door.

"Francesca! Where on earth have you been?" She hurried down the stairs to help Francesca get out of her wet coat. Amelia looked at the wrecked umbrella in dismay.

"The aunties would have had a stroke if they'd known you were out in this storm."

"It was awful," Francesca admitted. "Please don't tell them."

"I won't," Amelia readily agreed, taking the broken umbrella. "I'll hide this until we can throw it away."

"Good. Look what I bought." Francesca proudly displayed the fashion magazines.

"Ohhh, how nice. You dry off and I'll make some coffee and meet you in the living room and we can plan our wardrobes for the season."

Francesca and Amelia sat up late into the night discussing the expensive dresses. Although the walk in the rain had had its drawbacks, with the alarming winds and lightning, and Francesca's embarrassing encounter with the intimidating stranger, it had all been worth it. The rain had washed away the specters that had threatened to engulf her in the dark vault of self-pity. It was a path that she was desperately trying not to travel and she felt pleased that she had overcome the demeaning urge.

Francesca laughed suddenly and pointed to the clock. "Look at the time, Amelia. You have to go to work in the morning."

Amelia glanced up from her magazine. "My goodness, where did the time go? And I barely know what evening gowns I'm ordering from Paris. Tut-tut!" She primped her hair. "Not to worry, there's always tomorrow."

They laughed gaily and secured the house for the night. Without trying to put it into words, the two young women knew what they had missed all of their lives—the companionship of a sister to share things with.

Chapter Three

The aftermath of the storm left piles of bright leaves strewn over the streets and lawns with newly naked tree branches waving gently against a clear blue October sky. The warm rays of an Indian summer sun still beamed down on Edgecombe.

"Are you ready, Francesca?" Amelia called as Francesca took a last gulp of coffee.

"Coming," she answered, and kissed Daisy and Lelia quickly on the cheeks.

"Be careful," Lelia called to the two young women as they disappeared through the door.

Amelia backed the little foreign car out of the driveway and drove at a rapid clip into town. There were no clients waiting in the efficient real estate office when they arrived.

"We can have a few moments with Mr. Benson." Amelia knocked on a door that sat in a small alcove.

"Come in," a friendly voice answered in response to the knock.

''Good morning, Mr. Benson. I've brought Francesca to see you.''

''Fine.'' Mr. Benson rose from his comfortable old leather chair while Francesca waited for him to remember her. He only extended his hand and said, ''Hello, Francesca. Amelia's told me about you.'' Mr. Benson was a tall man with a lanky build and nice twinkle in his eyes that showed a shrewdness flecked with kindness behind gold-rimmed glasses. Francesca was much relieved when she found that she would not have to rack her brain to find Mr. Benson lost somewhere in her childhood memory.

Mr. Benson immediately got down to the purpose of Francesca's visit as he propped himself on the edge of his worn oak desk, offering Francesca and Amelia a seat. ''Florence will be with us another two or three months. Then you can start.''

Francesca breathed an sigh of relief. Mr. Benson had hired her without the usual long, laborious interview. He continued laying out his plans.

''There is a school over in Eton where you can take some classes.'' He gave Francesca a candid smile. ''If you're going to sell houses, you may as well know what you're talking about.''

Francesca was shown around the office and given some necessary papers that she was to fill out and Amelia showed her some books with listings of properties that were for sale. Shortly afterward, Amelia's clients arrived, anxious to see the houses that she had lined up for them. So they left Francesca in front of the real estate office. She looked up and down Main Street, wondering what she would do on her first day on her own.

The balmy air stirred her hair gently about her face. Her expression was now beginning to lose some of the tenseness that had pervaded it for the last few weeks.

In her aimless wandering around town, Francesca found herself on the beach, just about where she and Amelia had spent yesterday afternoon. She walked along the beach in the direction of the Lynche and English houses. She had the strange feeling that the houses were drawing her to them. She stood in awe before Isabel Lynche's house with its grand Palladian window staring blankly over the bay. She shuddered at the sight, and thought about how happiness had once reigned here.

Francesca withdrew her woeful gaze from the forlorn house, walking away until she came to the English house. It, too, stared out over the bay with emptiness.

The breeze from the water caught the almost-naked branches of the old trees and turned Francesca's gaze to an old brick wall with an arched entranceway. She walked hesitantly onto the smooth carpet of grass, soon coming upon a gravel path. She was startled when an old man appeared from behind some shrubbery carrying a pair of hedge shears. He glared at her suspiciously through tired old eyes.

"T'ain't nobody here, Miss."

Flustered at being caught on the property, Francesca quickly tried to explain to the man. "I'm terribly sorry. I'm Francesca Mayhew. I wasn't looking for anyone, I saw how beautiful the house was and came up for a closer look.'' The man still eyed her with suspicion. ''Perhaps you know my aunts, Lelia and Daisy Gaylord.'' She watched him with a sprinkling of hope.

''Oh, yeah. I know Miss Leila and Miss Daisy. Knowed 'em for years.'' Francesca was pleased to see that he was loosening up a bit.

''You must be Miz Rebecca's girl.''

''Yes.'' She smiled.

''Sorry to hear about your mom and dad.'' He spoke coolly but sincerely.

''Thank you—''

''Cyrus, Miss. Just old Cyrus.'' His voiced echoed pain. He looked about him. ''Nobody here, so ain't much to do. Thought I'd get some of the leaves up after last night's storm.''

Francesca could tell that that was a dismissal, so she backed away and said, ''I'm so glad to have met you, Cyrus, and thank you.'' She walked back across the sweeping lawn back down to the beach. She heard Cyrus say in the distance, almost to himself, ''Good-bye, Miss.''

She turned to see Cyrus holding his shears poised to cut the hedge as he peered curiously after her.

In her haste to get away from old Cyrus, Francesca thought that she was taking the same route back that had led her to the garden wall, but she found the path unfamiliar. She wound her way through the shrubbery. She could feel the breeze of the bay upon her face, so she knew that she was at least going in the right direction to the beach. She made a turn around a giant rhododendron and her breath stopped at the most beautiful sight she had ever seen. In all her travels, there had been nothing to compare to this almost unearthly sight.

An old road with long blades of brown grass growing in the center of sandy furrows led to a gray, weathered log fence laden with late-blooming pink roses twining around its post. In a frame of green rhododendrons sat the *Sea Song,* dancing on the gently splashing waves.

Francesca stood for a few moments in wonder at the beauty before her. She climbed between the posts to the other side. As she stared at the *Sea Song,* she felt an overwhelming desire to cry, and she closed her eyes to hold back the tears that swam there. She opened them again and the tears had vanished. She continued to walk along the beach. *Why is life so sad?* she thought. Away from the *Sea Song,* Francesca sat down on the sand and looked back at the boat. She jumped with a start at the sound of a voice from behind her.

"Beautiful day."

"Yes, it is," she answered the voice, looking up and shading her eyes with her hand. She saw a tall young man with very dark, almost black hair. He peered down at her with narrowed blue eyes the color of cornflowers.

"I was admiring the boat over there. It's hauntingly beautiful," she said, making conversation.

The young man's eyes turned in the direction of the *Sea Song.* "Yes, she is." He squatted down beside her. "Are you from around here?" he asked.

"I was born here, but I've never really lived in Edgecombe for any length of time, I'm afraid." She tilted her head and looked curiously at the man, who seemed, in spite of his friendly chatter, to be regarding her rather strangely.

"I'm Francesca Mayhew." She waited for him to give his name, but he looked out over the bay.

Finally he said, "Mine's Bud."

"How do you do?" The diplomatic world had taught Francesca the art of being gracious in difficult moments.

"Hi," he replied absently.

Francesca looked around and asked, "Do you live around here?"

"No. No, I don't." His gaze was still on the water.

She stood up and said, "It was nice meeting you. I must leave now."

The stranger rose from the sand, dusted the seat of his jeans, and said, "You, too. See you around."

Francesca made her way back to town. She took a last look at the *Sea Song* and looked back to see if the man was still on the beach, but just as he had appeared from nowhere, he had apparently vanished the same way.

Francesca found Daisy working in the garden, her large figure kneeling, bent over a flower bed, spading up soil. She heard Francesca come through the iron gate as it clanged behind her.

"Ah, Francesca, how did it go with William Benson?"

"Fine. I'll take some classes in Eton and start work when Florence leaves."

Daisy heaved herself up with the aid of Francesca. Removing her garden gloves, she gave the freshly turned-up mounds of earth a critical eye.

"I want to get the tulip bulbs in before it gets too cold."

"I'll change and help you."

"No, dear. I think I have gotten them all in. Have you had any lunch?"

"No, I wasn't very hungry." Francesca put her arm through her aunt's as they walked into the house.

"Ruth!" Daisy called as she hung her old gardening sweater in the hall closet.

Francesca thought of telling her aunts about the young man she had met on the beach, but fearing disapproval for talking to a stranger, she did not mention the incident until Amelia arrived home that evening.

Francesca and Amelia almost emulated their aunts in their evening gathering, talking about things that had happened during the day over a cup of coffee, but Francesca did mention Cyrus at dinner.

"I took a walk along the beach after I left you this morning, Amelia. I passed Lyre Hall and for some unknown reason, I walked up to Belle Rose and met the old gardener, Cyrus. I don't think he was too pleased with my boldness, going onto the grounds." She smiled.

"Poor old Cyrus. He gets around that place like a lost soul, as if he's waiting for everyone to come back.'' An unwelcomed tear glistened for a moment in Lelia's eyes as she tried to recover from her deep compassion for old Cyrus and the days they had shared and remembered.

''I suppose he'll stay on until they decide what's to be done with the house,'' Daisy said.

''Who will decide that?'' Francesca asked.

''Oh, Fergus and Axel Kingsly,'' Daisy replied.

''But what about Keal English's father?'' Francesca asked with concern.

''Well, Colin never cared that much for Belle Rose, and after Beth died, he really wanted no part of Edgecombe.'' Daisy sighed. ''And he's made English his home. Oh, he came and helped in the search for Keal, but he left again right after they gave up the search. But Keal loved Belle Rose and for some reason would never allow anyone to touch Lyre Hall.'' Daisy sighed again. ''He did love Isabel. Oh, how he loved her.''

After dinner, when they had all helped clear the dishes, the four women sat for a while in the drawing room and chatted about small, insignificant things of the day. But the conversation at the dinner table had left Daisy and Lelia thoughtful, and they soon took their leave and went to bed.

''I met a very handsome man on the beach today,'' Francesca said to Amelia over a cup of coffee.

''Who was he?'' Amelia asked with a gleam in her large dark eyes.

''I don't know. He said his name was Bud. He's not from here.''

"Are you going to see him again?" Mischief now played in Amelia's eyes.

"No, he didn't seem that interested."

"Oh, too bad. But who knows, Edgecombe is small and you might run into him again." Amelia spoke hopefully.

"It doesn't matter, really, but he seemed a little odd."

"Well, best you don't see him again if he's odd. It's bad enough when you *know* them and they're odd, but I don't recommend any odd strangers."

"I didn't mention it to the aunties." Francesca smiled knowingly at Amelia.

"Best not to," Amelia agreed through a gulp of coffee. "Aunt Lelia and Aunt Daisy are a little old-fashioned." She gave Francesca a knowing grin. "To say the least." She stared up at the ceiling. "Family, schooling, place of employment, etc., etc."

"You can't say that I'm not perceptive." Francesca laughed.

Becoming serious for a moment, Francesca said, "Thank you for getting the job for me. I think I'm going to like it. I called the school in Eton and made an appointment and can start classes on Tuesday."

"Good. That's all settled. Any good old movies on television tonight?"

The rest of the week went by fairly quickly for Francesca as she reacquainted herself with Edgecombe and helped Daisy in the garden. One afternoon, with nothing left to do, Francesca decided to explore the attic. She switched on the light at the foot of the stairs and made her way up the dimly lighted steps. All the wood had been left in its original state and had not been touched since the house had been built. The smell of old wood permeated the room.

There was another light at the top of the stairs and Francesca switched it on. The huge room came to life as the overhead globe flooded the room with light. Francesca was overwhelmed with what she saw. The room was filled with toys of bygone years. There were china dolls with blue glass eyes, dressed in white silk-and-lace dresses that were turning yellow with age. Straw hats trimmed with silk ribbons and flowers adorned the heads of the dolls, whose long dark curls hung over their tiny shoulders. Francesca's eyes were wide with wonder and surprise as she scanned the toys that were collected in a broad corner of the room. There were dollhouses—some were Victorian with gaslights and some were Colonial with bright-colored shutters. What fascinated Francesca most was a gaily painted merry-go-round.

Francesca spent the rest of the afternoon lost in the wonders of childhood toys of many, many years ago. She brushed the collected dust from an old wicker Victorian doll carriage that held a wooden doll with movable joints and a painted face. She was not very pretty but Francesca liked her and took her downstairs with her.

''I see you've found Beck.'' Daisy smiled at the sight of the old doll.

''What lovely toys. Are they from your childhood?'' Francesca asked with the excitement of a child.

"Yes, and some are older than that. We've kept them for many years," Daisy spoke nostalgically.

"May I keep Beck in my room?" she asked.

"Of course, dear. I think she needs some new clothes, though." Daisy laughed, cradling Beck with fond memories flooding her mind.

"I can't sew anything but buttons, and hardly that," Francesca admitted.

"I'll ask Ruth. She would probably like to make a doll's dress again."

"Good evening, everyone." Amelia burst through the door on a waft of cold air and elated spirits. "Guess who sold the old Mercer house?" She giggled happily.

Chapter Four

On Tuesday morning Francesca took the bus across the bay to Eton. The town was larger than Edgecombe and had more of a city air, with hurrying pedestrians and stained gray brick buildings that housed places of business. Many more automobiles filled the streets and honked noisily in exasperation at passing pedestrians and vexation at one another.

Francesca found her way along the main street of Eton, which did not have the charming shops selling antiques, bright linens, quaint books, and herbs. It did have what could only be described as small department stores, whose windows were decorated with mannequins dressed in less-than-fashionable clothes.

Francesca stopped to look in the windows for a moment and had a sudden desire to be surrounded by the charm and tranquility of Edgecombe. She sighed and thought that she should be able to stand Eton for a few months, if she tried hard. She turned from the store window and walked a little further up the street to find the building that housed her school.

Francesca found her first class interesting and learned some things about selling houses that she had never dreamed existed. She liked her new class-mates and she had been pleased with her day. Her thoughts as she walked to the bus that would take her back to Edgecombe gave a happy bounce to her step.

She was suddenly startled to hear her name called from behind and turned quickly to see who in the world knew her in Eton.

"Hello. I thought I recognized you from the restaurant window."

Francesca was indeed surprised to see Bud stand-ing before her. His narrow cornflower-blue eyes held a glint of mischief as he gazed at her.

"Hello—Bud, isn't it?" Francesca smiled pleas-antly at the young man, hoping that she was dis-playing only a mild sense of pleasure at seeing him again and not the overreaction of her heart beating rapidly in her chest.

"Where are you off to in such a rush?" he asked.

"Back to Edgecombe. The bus station is just up the street."

Bud pushed his hands deep into the pockets of the short leather jacket that he wore and looked at her with a mock pleading in his blue eyes. "I don't sup-pose there is any way that I can persuade you to miss your bus and have lunch with me?"

"Well . . ." She thought for a moment. "There's no reason to hurry back, I suppose." She smiled brightly at him and said, "I'd like to have lunch with you."

"Today is my lucky day." He grinned and guided her back to the restaurant where he had first caught sight of her from the window.

The restaurant was a place where the workers in town gathered. It smelled of tap beer and roast beef, with tables that were covered in red-and-white checkered cloths. The bartender was kept busy drawing beer for men who stood around in dingy work clothes. Bud pulled a chair out for Francesca and then sat down opposite her. A waiter brought them a menu and, without salutation, poised his pencil over a pad and asked, "What'll you have?"

Bud looked up at the waiter and said, "Hold on a minute and let the lady decide."

"Okay, buddy. I'll be back in a minute." The waiter walked off to serve a group of working men who had just arrived in loud and high spirits, glad for a break in their long workday.

"Now," Bud said over the din of noise that rose in the room, "what would you like?"

The menu was limited and Francesca chose a stew with a glass of red wine. Bud had the stew with a glass of beer.

Noticing Bud's dungarees and heavy work shoes, Francesca asked, "Do you work nearby?

His eyes flickered for a moment and he replied, "Yeah. Down on the docks."

"Are you a longshoreman?"

"Sort of, I guess." The same thoughtful look came into his eyes that she had noticed before, and she hoped that he did not think that his occupation would make a difference to her. The look had been fleeting and he was again almost, if not quite, jovial.

Francesca told Bud of her experiences in all the countries where her father had served, and he laughed heartily when she told him how once an employee had taken her and another daughter of a diplomat sailing, and how she had fallen overboard in the dangerous lake that contained every horrible thing that lived in water.

"Poor Jamil. He was yelling and screaming the whole time he was fishing me out of the lake."

In a more serious tone Bud said, "But you were all right?"

"Oh, yes, but I thought we would have to bury Jamil."

They ate their lunch slowly. The once-crowded restaurant dissolved into near emptiness as the workers gradually returned to their labors, announcing that the lunch hour had come to a close. Dreading the moment when they would have to go their separate ways, the young couple continued to talk. Finally feeling a bit guilty about keeping Bud, Francesca asked, "Don't you have to go back to work?"

Bud toyed for a moment with his coffee spoon and replied, "No, there's not much unloading to do on the docks of Eton." He looked at his watch and playfully said, "I have some bad news for you."

Surprise reflected in Francesca's warm brown eyes. "What is it?"

"You've missed your bus back to Edgecombe."
He continued to grin at her mischievously. "Now
you will have to take the five-thirty bus."

Francesca hurriedly fished around in her purse for
change to telephone her aunt. "Oh, I must call
home. My aunts will be worried. Is there a telephone
here?"

"Over in the corner. Do you see where that man
in the red cap is standing?"

"Yes, I'll be back in a moment." Francesca disappeared behind the man in the red cap and soon
emerged again with a smile on her face.

"All right?" Bud asked.

"All right. They will hold dinner for me." And
for no reason they both started to laugh.

"Come on, let's walk along the bay until it's time
for your bus," Bud said, leaving the money with the
bill and tip on the table. "You've had better
lunches," he said as they left the tavern.

"I found it rather tasty and hearty." She smiled
up at Bud.

"And the company?" he asked.

"Delightful," she replied, laughing.

Bud led Francesca down to the wharf and they
strolled along down to the sandy shore. The sun became a yellow ball in the early gathering dusk and
was slowly descending into the bay, painting the
gently rippling waters a radiant shimmering gold.
The infinite sky was streaked with purple and gold
with tints of salmon as gulls whirled overhead, their
far cry bidding the sun good night, mingled with the
calm lapping of the water as it touched the shore.

Francesca stooped and picked up a crimson leaf that floated on the water.

"How pretty," she said, holding the leaf for Bud to see. He smiled at her and they continued their walk in silence, with the secret longing to touch each other flowing between them. If Bud had reached for Francesca's hand it would not have been the hand of a stranger. The golden light that had beamed so warmly on their faces a few short moments ago was now a cool, deepening blue. Bud looked at his watch again. "I think we had better get you back to your bus. We don't want to upset your aunts."

Walking back to the bus, mostly in silence, Francesca tried to deal with the awful panic of worrying that Bud might make no arrangements to see her again. The thought kept Francesca's mind occupied until they reached the bus station. The bus was already there. She stopped before they reached the door of the bus and held out her hand to Bud and said calmly, "Thank you so much for a lovely afternoon." He took her hand and held it for a moment.

"When is your next class?"

"On Friday." Her heart quickened its beat.

"Will you have lunch with me again? Same place? Same time?"

"Yes, I'd like that."

"Good. But I won't promise to get you on the three-thirty bus."

Francesca's only reply to that was a pleased smile. She got onto the bus and took a seat by the window to wave good-bye to Bud as he waited on the platform. She watched him from the window, still standing, looking after the bus until it was far up the street. She saw him turn and walk back in the direction that they had come, and she suddenly felt a great pity for Bud, because for some reason he seemed so alone. She reasoned that perhaps that was just her imagination, but she felt alive again, and, she mused, even happy again.

Francesca walked from the bus stop up the hill to Holly Street with a real bounce in her footsteps. Her dark hair, flouncing in the evening breeze, flowed back from a lovely face that was illuminated by the prospect of love.

She tried to still the rapture that was coursing through her as she let herself in through the door. Feeling a bit of guilt, she called cheerfully in the entrance hall, ''Hello, everyone, I'm home.''

Daisy came to meet her. ''Hello, dear, you're just in time for dinner.''

Later that evening, after Daisy and Lelia had retired to their rooms, Francesca and Amelia made a pot of coffee and sat in the drawing room to go over the events of their day.

''I saw Bud today in Eton. We had lunch.'' Francesca looked for approval from Amelia and she got it.

''Really, is he very nice?'' she asked, her eyes dancing with mischievous anticipation. ''When will you see him again?'' Amelia ran on.

''Friday. I'm going to have lunch with him again after my class,'' Francesca spoke dreamily. ''Oh,

Amelia, we walked along the bay in the setting sun.''

"I do believe, Francesca Mayhew, that you are falling in love."

"Don't be silly. No, I just like him," Francesca said defensively. "I don't even know him."

"Well, I'm glad it's Friday that you're meeting him, because Saturday we are invited to dinner at Charlotte's. She's going to introduce you to Edgecombe society." Her eyes rolled up to the ceiling, then she looked thoughtful for a moment. "Are you going to tell them about Bud? What does he do, anyway?"

Francesca bit her bottom lip. "I think he works on the docks."

"A *longshoreman?*" Amelia's voice squeaked. "Charlotte would love that. Don't mention him just yet, even to the aunties." The same devilish spark appeared in her eyes again. "A longshoreman. Francesca, how exciting." Amelia curled her arms around her drawn-up knees. "You know, of course, that as soon as Aunt Lelia and Aunt Daisy know that you are meeting a young man, they will want you to bring him home to dinner."

"I know. I think he will be our secret for a while longer." Francesca smiled happily at Amelia.

On Friday, Francesca finished her class and, with an eager heart, hurried off to meet Bud at Lacy's Tavern. She now held the name of the tavern with a special endearment, with all its lack of style and elegance—its sawdust-covered floor and the cool smell of beer on tap, mixed with the aroma of pick-les in barrels of brine. It would always be close to her heart because this was as near to heaven as she had ever been.

Wild thoughts began to invade her mind as she hurried along the autumn sun-bathed street. *What if Bud has forgotten?* She hadn't spoken to him since she had left him at the bus station. What if he simply just didn't show up? Francesca's legs were becom-ing heavy and her footsteps slowed under the burden of doubt that was now running helter-skelter through her head. She turned the corner onto Pike Street where she saw the dusty green awning flapping in the Indian summer breeze. She could see no sign of anyone waiting in front of the tavern.

With a fluttering heart filled with anxiety that was rising to panic, Francesca approached Lacy's. Just as she touched the old curved handle of the screen door, it pushed open and Bud walked through. He carried a large brown cardboard box in his arms. When he saw her he broke into a big grin. Shifting the box up under his arm, looking up at the bright blue sky that was feathered with downy white clouds, he said, ''The day is much too beautiful to sit in a dark dank room, don't you think? So I asked Tom to fix a picnic lunch and I've rented a sailboat. We can have lunch on the bay.'' He looked at her for approval. ''How does that sound to you?'' He grinned. ''And I promise not to let you fall into the water.''

''Oh, wonderful. What a lovely idea, Bud.'' She reached for the thermos jug that he held in his other hand. Walking jauntily down to the wharf, they found the little sailboat and shoved out into the bay.

Beams of sunlight flickered brilliant flashes of light from the gentle rippling waters, while overhead white clouds of silk floss floated under a cerulean blue sky. And Francesca's joy was brighter than the day itself.

Bud took out two roast beef sandwiches, placed them on heavy duty china plates, and opened a bottle of red wine. He unwrapped two bar-style wine-glasses. Holding them up proudly, he said, "Tom lent me these."

After they had eaten they both lay back and let the sunlight and bay breeze play upon their faces while they listened to the soft lapping of the water and dreamed. The boat drifted along by itself. Bud sat up and gazed down at Francesca. His shadow fell across her face and she opened her eyes and found Bud's blue eyes peering down into hers as the wind tossed his black hair about his face. His voice was solemn when he spoke. "I'm so glad that I met you, Francesca." He reached over and gently brushed back the strands of her hair that were blowing into her face.

"So am I, Bud."

He touched her face, caressing it softly, and Francesca could feel the roughness of the calluses on his hands. Francesca removed Bud's hands from her face and examined them tenderly. She then raised them to her soft full lips and kissed each one lightly. No longer able to hold back his love for Francesca, Bud swept her into his arms and their lips met, uniting two souls in the bond of love. They soared with the seagulls who sang a love song in the long shadows of the sun as they whirled gracefully on the wind. The two new lovers sat for a long time in the silent joy of being together. Francesca's head leaned on Bud's shoulder as he held her in the warmth of his arms.

They gazed across the bay where a thin mist was beginning to rise. Francesca rose out of Bud's protective arm and peered into the distance.

"There's the *Sea Song*." A look of sadness reflected on Francesca's lovely face as she watched the boat with its sails furled. "It's so sad. So very sad. My friend, Amelia, says that the *Sea Song* waits for Keal English. But I guess he won't come back to her."

"What do you know of this English fellow?" Bud asked as if there might have been a hint of jealousy.

"Oh, I didn't know him, although Amelia said that I had met him as a child, but I don't remember him. His aunt was a very close friend of my two aunts who I'm living with now. So they are quite upset over all of this."

"I'm sorry for your aunts," he said sincerely, looking again up at the sky that was beginning to have streaks of gold. The gulls, with carefree abandon, loitered over the calm water as the sun cast long shadows.

"I guess I had better get you back to shore so that you can make the five-thirty bus." He unfurled the sail and hoisted it up to the wind for the sail back to the wharf.

This time they held hands as they walked to the bus station, and Bud kissed Francesca good-bye as she got on the bus. He waited until the bus left the station before he left to go ''who knows where,'' Francesca thought as she watched him walk away. She pictured Bud going to some lonely room in a neighborhood that was not very nice and she wondered how they would resolve their lives. She didn't know what would happen, but she knew that she wanted to be with him and she could hardly wait until Tuesday when she would see Bud again at Lacy's. Even though this excited Francesca, she knew that their meeting just at Lacy's on the day of her classes could not go on forever. At some point she would have to introduce him to her aunts, but first, she would let Amelia meet him so that she would have some support if her aunts objected to Bud's occupation.

Chapter Five

Saturday was spent getting ready for Charlotte's dinner party. If Francesca had little else, she did have a splendid wardrobe, which she and Amelia went through with Amelia choosing an evening dress that she liked and Francesca giving it to her. It had been a dress that she and her mother had bought in Paris on one of their R and Rs. Francesca smiled; they did everything but rest and relax.

At 7:00 they were dressed and ready. Francesca wore a white chiffon gown that flowed from a gathering at the waist and a fluid cape of fluttering chiffon tied loosely in a bow draped down around her shoulders in the style of the thirties. Her dark hair, hanging loosely around her shoulders, was caught on each side with exquisite gold combs embellished with tiny gold flowers with diamond chips in the center of each blossom. Francesca appraised herself in the mirror and her lips puckered into a pout. Though pleased at her reflection, it hardly mattered

46

how well she looked; Bud would not be there for her to proudly show off to.

The four ladies met in the entrance hall, all looking their very best. Lelia wore a black silk taffeta gown that swished on the air when she walked. It had ruffled cuffs and a ruffled high neck where she wore her pride and joy, the Victorian cresent-shaped diamond brooch. Her blue-white hair was waved back from her face and twisted in a French roll.

Daisy's gown was of indigo blue silk floral print with pink and yellow roses trailing through it on green vines. A thin chiffon coat of the same print with long puffed sleeves was worn over the gown.

Amelia was the last to come down and she looked lovely in a silk chiffon gown of a pale pink with a halter neckline that wrapped around into a sash. Her simple gold sandals glittered under her hem and she wore her hair pulled back with an Edwardian pink rose.

The two aunts beamed their pride on the two young women who stood before them.

"Aunt Lelia and Aunt Daisy, you look absolutely beautiful." Francesca looked lovingly at the two old ladies.

The sound of the doorbell sent them all rushing for their wraps and the door as Charlotte's driver waited to take them to the Moores'. As they were going down the steps, Francesca whispered to Amelia, "I hope that Charlotte invited Bill Adams. You seem to like him, from the way you looked when you told me about him."

Amelia blushed. "I doubt he's invited. He's not

what Charlotte would consider 'of the right family background.' To her, he's merely a real estate salesman.''

They stepped into the limousine. Francesca was surprised at Amelia's comment, and she thought, *What would Charlotte think of Bud, a man who works with his hands, a manual laborer?*

The car swung around an iron gate and up a crescent driveway to a splendid house that sat on a hill overlooking Edgecombe. Yellow lights glowed from the windows of the house which was silhouetted against the dark sky where clouds were gathering. The chauffeur helped Lelia and Daisy to the door, which was opened by a butler.

''Good evening, Miss Daisy, Miss Lelia.'' He took their wraps.

''Good evening, Simon,'' Leila said, and Daisy greeted him with, ''Good to see you looking so well, Simon.''

''Thank you, Miss Daisy.'' Simon smiled, pleased with Daisy's warm greeting. He then went to the young women who were standing aside.

''Good evening, Miss Amelia. Ahem.'' Simon was waiting for someone to give him a hint as to the identity of Francesca as he said, ''Good evening, Miss.''

''Oh, Simon, this is Miss Francesca Mayhew. She is the niece of Miss Lelia and Miss Daisy,'' Amelia informed him.

''Good evening, Miss.'' He bowed stiffly.

''Hello, Simon,'' Francesca acknowledged the introduction. At that moment Charlotte appeared in the doorway of the drawing room. She glanced up the graceful stairway and came to meet Daisy and Lelia.

"Hello, my dears. Jeffers got you here all right, I see. Fergus hasn't come down yet, but most of the guests have arrived."

Charlotte looked impeccable, as usual. Her pale blond hair, which no doubt would have been gray without the expert champagne tinting by her hairdresser, was flawlessly coiffed. A double strand of large luminous pearls were draped over her matronly bosom.

"I've invited some eligible young men who you young ladies might find interesting," Charlotte said, glancing back over her shoulder at Francesca and Amelia. Looking very pleased, she tipped elegantly with short steps with all the grace that her beautiful pearl-gray silk dress, with its narrow hem, would allow her. She led them into the drawing room where the other guests waited. Men in black tie rose from their chairs when they entered the room. Others stood at the fireplace chatting about business affairs. The eyes of the young men whom Charlotte had mentioned became keenly alert when Francesca and Amelia walked into the room. What their heightened senses did not tell them was that neither Amelia nor Francesca would have any interest in them whatsoever as they stood eagerly awaiting their turn to be introduced. Even if there had been an outside chance of Francesca finding one of them interesting, Amelia already knew her fate for the evening. She knew all of them and the evening was already growing long.

The young men were showing the usual male display of strutting before a pretty girl when Fergus entered with Axelrod Kingsly.

Fergus was a round little man with a fringe of gray hair circling around his ears. His silver-rimmed glasses and sparse hair curling up in the center of his head gave him the comical look of a Dickens character. He came toward Francesca with outstretched hands. Grasping her hands, he spread their arms out as he scrutinized her from head to toe.

"Aahhh, Francesca." He turned to Charlotte. "Hasn't she grown into a beautiful young lady? Francesca, the boys in this town are going to pile themselves on your doorstep." The young men standing around beamed and hung onto every word that Fergus said.

"I'm sure they will. That's why I invited the nicest ones tonight." Charlotte's eyes demurely scanned the young men as they grinned broadly at the smug flattery. Charlotte interrupted Fergus's somewhat winded adulation of Francesca.

"Francesca, my dear, let me introduce you to Axel Kingsly. Axel is the Chief Counsel for English Shipping."

"Well, I have heard nothing but praise for you, Francesca."

"You're very kind, Mr. Kingsly." Francesca rather liked Mr. Kingsly. He was tall and distinguished looking, with thinning gray hair and a small mustache. He had the confident air of a diplomat who always knew the right words to say to whomever he was speaking at the moment. He shook Francesca's hand warmly.

"And Francesca, you've met Ophelia Defoe. This is her husband, Dr. Robert Defoe." Dr. Defoe was an attractive man with graying hair that had once been carrot color, with a few freckles and warm brown eyes. The hand that he extended was strong in its grip and was covered with freckles. Ophelia stood aside, looking on her husband with obvious love and pride. She moved toward Daisy and put her arm through Daisy's and they walked over to the sofa and sat down, chatting intimately, with Ophelia leaning forward in her chair speaking softly so the others might not hear as she reached over and patted Daisy's hand.

At that moment the butler entered the door and announced that dinner was served. The guests paired off, with Daisy on the arm of Dr. Defoe and Lelia on the arm of Fergus. The young men were disappointed when Axel Kingsly offered his arm to Francesca. One alert young man rushed to the side of Amelia and offered her his arm.

Axel Kingsly's wife went in with another of the executives and each followed with a partner to the dining room. When a sudden draft of cold air swept over them, Charlotte turned to see the butler open the door. Francesca's and Amelia's eyes followed the direction of the wind and both were surprised to see Bill Adams hurry in.

"Sorry I'm late, Mrs. Moore," he apologized sheepishly as he handed his overcoat to the butler and joined them in the procession to the dining room.

Surprise and gladness sparkled in Amelia's eyes.

Francesca turned and gave Amelia a knowing smile. Amelia tried to treat the issue with a cool nonchalance as she stumbled slightly on the doorstep. Francesca averted her head and held back a laugh.

Charlotte seated everyone in their proper places. Unfortunately, Bill was seated down the table across from Amelia, but he managed to steal a few glances at her. Francesca was seated next to a very boring young man who seemed to have no conversation about anything other than who the right people were, and the right country club to belong to. Francesca's only thoughts were that any place this man was would be the wrong place for her. She smiled at him and stifled a yawn, which he never noticed. Her mind wandered to Bud as she looked intently at the young man and his voice faded from her mind as a fixed smile formed on her lips. She thanked the heavens for having been around diplomats; it trained one to be false graciously, and the young man whose voice droned on and on never knew that Francesca didn't hear a word he said.

She was brought back to the party when she heard a voice that turned out to be Dr. Defoe's ask Fergus, ''Any news of young English?''

''No, not a word. Sad, sad business.'' Fergus shook his head.

Someone else asked, ''What about the houses and his boat?''

''Heaven only knows what we will do about Belle Rose and Lyre Hall,'' Charlotte said. ''Keal would never allow anyone to touch Isabel's house. It has been the same since she died. An employee keeps it exactly as it was, as if he expected her to come back.'' Charlotte drew in a breath. ''And now he's gone. Life is so unreasonable. Such a young man, becoming a bit wild. . . .'' Her voice trailed off and picked up again. ''Just before the accident.''

Lelia's fork paused in midair and she looked curiously at Charlotte. ''Why, I never knew Keal to be wild,'' she stated, perplexed by this new revelation of Keal's character.

''Oh, I didn't want to worry you and Daisy, so I never said anything at all about it.''

Francesca thought that for a moment she saw Bill Adams wince while he continued his conversation with the young lady seated next to him.

After dinner the ladies retired to the sitting room and the men to the library.

''I know that a lot of young people think that men and women splitting up after dinner is silly, but we must remember that all etiquette had a practical beginning. It's just so the ladies and gentlemen can go to the rest room in comfort. So, ladies, the powder room is just around the corner.'' Charlotte pulled a silk cord by the fireplace and a maid soon entered the room.

''Agnes, would you serve coffee now, with sherry, please, and the gentlemen in the library with brandy?''

''Yes, ma'am.'' The maid left the room, shutting the door behind her.

Ophelia asked Charlotte, ''What made you say that Keal was wild?''

''Oh, the people he was going around with, particularly that girl, Donna Webster. Isabel would have had a fit.''

''I don't recall the girl being particularly wild. She just worked at Bailey's Five and Dime.''

''Well, Ophelia, I hardly think that it is suitable for a young man of Keal's social position to have been seen dating this girl. After all, next year he was to take over English Shipping.''

''Well, I hardly see—'' Ophelia was cut off by Charlotte's retort.

''I don't really expect you to understand, Ophelia.''

Ophelia's face flushed a deep red and she said, ''Excuse me. I must go to the powder room.''

The men soon joined the women and the conversation changed to more suitable topics, like garden clubs and the coming holidays. At 11:00 Lelia asked Charlotte to call the car and the dinner party ended. Not a dinner party that Francesca would hold in fond memories, but a disturbing one. She had found an undercurrent of animosity between Charlotte and Ophelia, though when she had first met them, they seemed congenial enough.

After Lelia and Daisy retired, Francesca sat on Amelia's bed and they talked.

''This was a rather strange evening.'' Francesca looked puzzled.

Amelia stretched and said, ''I think you're being kind. It was a rotten evening and that's an understatement.''

''It should have helped a bit having Bill Adams there.''

"It did, just a bit, though. You know, he's never asked me out. Modest as it might be, Bud does take you to lunch and, at least, you know that he cares something for you. But Bill . . .'' She spread her hands and shrugged her shoulders. "Is just there. I think he likes me, but I don't really know." She thought for a moment, a frown creasing her brow.

"It was really odd, Charlotte inviting Bill. She's a stickler for social standing and Bill isn't from the 'right family.' '' She lay across the bed. "You're right, it was a strange evening. Let's hope that Charlotte doesn't have any more dinner parties anytime soon."

"I like Fergus," Francesca said, questioning her own taste.

"Fergus is a nice little man."

"And Ophelia?"

"Ophelia is a real person. No phony airs. She just appeared in Edgecombe one day. She stayed with us for a while. Aunt Daisy found out that Dr. Defoe needed a secretary." Amelia smiled. "She got the job *and* the doctor. Charlotte tolerates Ophelia because the doctor is from one of Edgecombe's first families. She doesn't really approve of her."

"Oh, what webs we weave when we mind someone else's business," Francesca stated.

"Not very poetic, but true." Amelia smiled a sad smile. "Ophelia appeared here like me. I don't know where Ophelia came from and I don't know where I came from."

Francesca went to Amelia and put her arms around her. "Oh, Amelia, I know it must be hard, but I'm sure Aunt Lelia and Aunt Daisy will tell you when the time is right.'' Francesca frowned. ''Haven't they told you anything at all?''

''They said that I was staying with a friend, an old woman in the country, and she was no longer able to look after me, so they brought me to live with them.'' She smiled. ''They said because I was such a pretty little girl.''

''They were right.'' Francesca smiled back at Amelia. ''It will be all right, you will see.'' Francesca got up from the bed. ''I think it's time to go to bed and sleep Charlotte's party off. I hate to sound ungrateful.''

''But you didn't like the party.'' Amelia laughed.

''Right.'' Francesca also laughed. ''I'll send her a note tomorrow.'' When Francesca reached the door, she turned back to Amelia and said, ''Wherever you're from, Amelia, I'm glad you're here. I now have a sister.''

''Me, too,'' Amelia said.

Sunday seemed like an endless day. Daisy and Lelia went to church while Amelia and Francesca helped Ruth prepare an early Sunday dinner. Francesca washed her hair and wrote a thank-you note to Charlotte. Amelia asked her. ''Is there any chance Bud might call?''

''None. He doesn't know the number and he didn't ask for it, come to think of it.''

''Can you call him?''

Francesca suddenly looked aghast and spoke with

disbelief. ''You know, Amelia, I don't know his last name.''

Amelia almost did a double take. ''Really? I think you and Bud had better work on having a little better communication, don't you?''

''Oh, Amelia, he could disappear and I would never know where to find him or whom to ask.'' Francesca turned away from Amelia. She didn't want her to see the fear that was creeping over her as the dreaded thought rose in her heart. Suppose she went to Lacy's and Bud wasn't there? Perhaps Lacy would know. She realized for the first time that there was no common link between them, and she could lose him forever and never know why. Francesca suddenly sat down. The burden of fear was too much and she clasped her hands in her lap, like a forlorn old woman to whom life had dealt one blow too many. She looked up at Amelia with dull aching eyes filled with uncertainty.

''Bud will be there, Francesca.'' Amelia had understood the moment and wanted to calm Francesca's fears, and she repeated, ''He will be there.''

Monday had been long and fitful for Francesca and her dreams had been strange and unsettling, with Bud fading away from her as she tried to reach him. She dressed quickly, glad that morning had finally arrived, but with its overcast gray skies, it did nothing in the way of reassuring her that her fears were groundless. She heard Amelia call her from the bottom of the stairs.

''Francesca, breakfast is ready. Hurry, I'll drop you off at the bus station.''

"Coming." She met Amelia on the steps. "I'm not very hungry. I'll just have a cup of coffee and be with you in a minute." She almost ran to the kitchen where Ruth was pouring her coffee. She was glad that Lelia and Daisy had not come down yet.

If only the day had been bright and gloriously sunny instead of gray and dreary with the naked branches of the trees showing even more, with most of their leaves now strewn aimlessly about the grounds.

The bus pulled into the station and Francesca got off feeling even more dejected. Sometime today the moment of truth would come, she thought. As she stepped down she heard someone say, "Hi!" She looked up and there stood Bud. If her heart had had a voice, it would have burst into song as doubt blew away like fog on a fresh wind.

"Oh, Bud." And the dull lifeless look of despair lifted from Francesca's face like a veil revealing a radiant glow of love.

"Come on, I'll carry your books." He smiled. "You know. . . ." His voice trailed off.

Francesca looked up at him with a beaming face, waiting for him to finish what he had started to say. When it was apparent that he would not go on, she asked, "Do I know what?"

"Ah, nothing."

"Oh." Francesca wondered what made him change his mind.

"I won't be able to have lunch with you today. I

have to work. A ship's come in and we have to unload her.''

''Oh.'' Disappointment rang in Francesca's voice.

''Oh, don't sound that way. I'll make it up to you. How about dinner on Wednesday?''

''I'd like that.'' She brightened up.

''Good. How shall we meet?'' He saw how pleased she was, and grinned down at her with the gratification that he pleased her.

''Would you like to come to Edgecombe and meet my family?'' Francesca thought now would be as good a time as ever to introduce Bud to her aunts.

''If you don't mind, Francesca, I'd rather meet you here in Eton. I'll probably have to work that day.'' He smiled at her again. ''And I'll want to go home and spruce up a bit.'' He playfully bumped into her, his dark hair falling over his eyes. ''For my big date.''

''All right,'' Francesca agreed, with an unseen shrug and the thought, *If not now, soon.* They had arrived at the school before she realized it. Bud returned her books to her.

''Be a good girl, and do as the teacher tells you.''

Francesca laughed at his silliness. ''I will.''

Bud's blue eyes suddenly turned serious. He gazed into Francesca's lovely clear walnut eyes and gently took her face in his hands and kissed her on the forehead. ''What time will you come in on Wednesday?''

''Is seven all right?'' she asked.

"Fine. I'll be there." As Francesca started through the door, Bud called to her.

"Francesca." She turned back to him. "I'll always be there."

Walking up the steps to her class, she wondered how had he known her fears. Aghast, she remembered she still did not know his last name.

Chapter Six

On Wednesday at 5:30, Amelia helped Francesca dress for her date with Bud. They tried to keep their excitement very low-key so that Lelia and Daisy would think that the occasion was of no great importance. Francesca had told a small white lie; she had said that she was going to dinner with some of her classmates in Eton. She knew that if she had told them that she was going on a date with a young man, they would have immediately wanted to know why he wasn't coming to call for her at home. Since she did not really know why, she couldn't give a reasonable explanation, and she was much too happy to have any doubts thrown on Bud's character.

Francesca put on a peach-colored angora sweater with a V neck and a peach skirt of soft wool crepe. She then put on very smart green lizard pumps; her small purse was of the same lizard skin with a thin gold chain shoulder strap.

"Francesca, you look fantastic," Amelia exclaimed.

"Do I really look all right?" Francesca asked, observing herself in the full-length mirror.

"Perfect. You'll knock Bud right off his feet." She swung herself off of Francesca's bed where she had been appraising her and said, "Come on, I'll drive you to the bus. I would offer to drive you to Eton, but I don't think Bud is ready to meet us." She thought for a moment. "Why don't you take the car?"

"Thanks, Amelia, but I don't have a U.S. license yet, or any license for that matter. Anyway, Bud's meeting me at the bus station."

Francesca went downstairs to the drawing room to get the approval of her aunts. She told them that she would be home around 11:00, and no later than 12:00. They gave their proud approval of their niece and said the usual things adults say to a young person whom they want to protect. She in turn promised to obey all of their wishes to be careful and not to stay out too late. She kissed them good night and joined Amelia in her little car with the engine already running.

When Francesca got on the bus the stars were already out and sparkling like dewdrops in a clear dark indigo autumn sky. Francesca glanced sidelong at her reflection in the dark window glass, hoping that nothing would go awry. She touched her thick dark hair, brushing it back into a better position. She would never be able to see herself as she truly was, flawlessly beautiful, and that it would have made very little difference if a few strands of her hair were out of place.

Bud was standing at the foot of the steps of the bus when she alighted, giving her an observant and pleased smile. He did not wear a coat, but was attired in a neat, well-cut navy blue suit, a white shirt with pale blue stripes, and a blue silk tie with small paisley designs of a reddish orange print. In her entire life Francesca thought she had never seen a man as handsome as Bud.

"You look lovely," he said, taking her by the arm guiding her out of the bus station. "I have a car over here." He took her to a small compact American car that was a dark red, shiny and new. When they were seated in the car, Francesca noticed that the car had a rental sticker in the left-hand corner of the windshield. Bud maneuvered the car expertly away from the curb and onto the street that led them on a road along the bay. They climbed steadily uphill on the dark road, the headlights bobbing on the asphalt, giving them the feeling of being the only two people in the world.

Francesca had no idea where they were going. She looked out over the vast span of the inky black bay that spread below them like a great dark void; tiny lights in the far distance twinkled along the shore of Edgecombe.

They had driven for miles along the dark winding road, mostly in silence, when Bud suddenly put the turn signal on and said, "Here we are."

Francesca saw a very impressive Colonial house that sat back from the road. It was white; she could tell because of floodlights that illuminated it. The shutters were dark, but she could not distinguish the

color. As Bud turned in, an old Colonial sign said
BROOK HOUSE. It looked very expensive. She turned
to Bud as he parked the car.

"Do you think we should go here?" She hoped
that she was being tactful. She did not want to hurt
Bud's feelings, but neither did she want him to
spend money that he might later regret when the
month's rent came due.

He smiled indulgently at her. "Of course we
should. I was paid quite well today and I want to
splurge on my lovely date." He got out of the car
and went to Francesca's door. She unlocked her door
reluctantly, still pondering Bud's decision. He
opened her door and took her hand, studying her for
a moment.

They were greeted at the entrance by a lovely
woman in a white silk blouse and black skirt holding
menus in her arms. She led them to a table in the
corner of the room, romantically set for two by the
window overlooking the bay. A lone candle burned
in a crystal candlestick, flickering its reflection in the
cobalt blue and gold-trimmed china, casting a warm
glow over the yellow and white wallpapered room.
The maître d' pulled out a Queen Anne chair for
Francesca, and when they were comfortably seated
she handed them each a menu, pointed out the dishes
she thought best tonight. Wishing them an enjoyable
meal, she departed and a waiter appeared shortly
with pad and pencil poised to take their order.

Francesca was careful not to order the most expensive dish, like lobster, even though Bud urged

her to have it. Instead, she ordered the *coq au vin*,
which was every bit as sublime.

They were seated next to a large window that
overlooked the dark bay where a few twinkling
lights sprinkled in the distance. Francesca gazed
around the room in admiration. Just behind Bud sat
an old hutch that held a large bouquet of yellow
chrysanthemums in a ceramic pot.

"This is a lovely place." She leaned back in the
chair feeling the quiet beauty of the restaurant. "Is
it a new restaurant?" she asked.

"I think it was new almost two hundred years
ago." Bud grinned at her. "It was an old stagecoach
stop and I believe its always been owned by the
same family."

"How marvelous. I love it."

"I'm glad," he looked pleased. "We can come
again."

"That sounds promising." She smiled at him.

"It is a promise." He said in a more serious tone
than she had expected.

With dinner finished, Francesca and Bud sat quietly talking over coffee and brandy as the evening
wore on. Bud had become more withdrawn and
twirled the stem of his brandy glass around silently.
Francesca could tell that his thoughts were disturbing him. He finally leaned across the table and took
her hands in his rough callused ones. Francesca's
heart went out to him at their touch. She wanted to
soothe the work-worn hands with tears and kisses,

but instead she only folded her graceful fingers over his and gently caressed them.

Bud drew in a breath and spoke. "Look, Francesca." At these words, Francesca's heart fluttered and dropped. She knew that she was about to hear something that she did not wish to hear.

"I've got to go to New York. There's some work there. I won't be gone very long."

"Oh," she heard herself say weakly.

"Don't look so sad. I said I'll be back soon, and I must go."

Those words seemed final to Francesca and she would not try to dissuade him from going, as much as she felt like pleading with him not to go away. She lowered her eyes and asked, "When will you return?"

"In a week or so." He gazed at her beseechingly for understanding, which he did not get.

Francesca thought that if he had said a week, he would have known exactly when he was going to return, but "in a week or so" rang with uncertainty.

"Can I know where you will be staying?" she asked dishearteningly.

"I don't know just yet where I'll be staying," he answered.

"Well, I guess I'll just have to wait until I hear from you."

"You'll hear from me."

"How?" Anger rose in her voice. "You don't have my phone number and you don't know where I live." She removed her hands from his and placed them in her lap.

''I'll know where you live tonight when I take you home.'' He smiled at her as one would a pouting child. ''Hmm?''

Francesca smiled suddenly. ''That's true.''

''You see''—Bud leaned toward her again, and humor had vanished from his eyes—''I want you to always remember that I might be late, but I will be there.'' He grinned at her, the humor back in his eyes. ''Okay?''

''Okay.'' She smiled back at him.

''What time did you tell your aunts you would be in?''

''Around eleven, no later than twelve.''

Bud consulted his watch, which looked expensive to Francesca. ''Well, it's eleven-twenty now, so it will have to be no later than twelve, Cinderella.'' He stood to help her from her chair. ''I must get you home on time or your aunts might not let you go out with me again.''

They don't know now, she thought to herself.

Francesca directed Bud to Holly Street, but he did not seem to need it very much.

''You seem to know Edgecombe,'' she said.

''I met you in Edgecombe.'' He turned to her and smiled. ''Remember?''

''Oh, yes.'' She smiled back at him. ''That's right.''

When they arrived at the house on Holly Street, Bud kissed her good night, quickly leaned over to her side of the car, and lifted the handle and opened the door for her to get out.

"I'll wait here until you get inside the house," he said.

Francesca was a little disappointed that Bud did not walk her to the door, and she thought that perhaps longshoremen had different sets of rules for manners. As she walked up the brick path, Bud called, "Francesca!" She turned to his call, and he said, "I'll be seeing you." She gave him a little wave of her hand and walked up the path. When she entered the door, she stood and watched him drive away.

So, without the benefit of the solemn vows of marriage and the joy of childbirth, Lelia and Daisy still bore the awesome burden of waiting for a beloved child to come in for the night. When Francesca stepped from the car, Lelia gave up her vigil at the window. She dropped the edge of the lace curtain that she held back for a clearer view of the street and wearily climbed into bed.

When Daisy heard Francesca come up the stairs, she put her book of poetry by Lord Byron on the night table and turned the light out and went to sleep.

Amelia had stayed awake, not from worry that something might happen to Francesca, but to be awake when she returned to find out all the wonderful things that had occurred on her grand date. So when Francesca reached the head of the stairs, Amelia was waiting and they quietly went into Francesca's room to analyze the events of the evening.

On Friday, Francesca halfheartedly went to her class in Eton. Knowing that Bud would not be there gave her absolutely no incentive to go to class. She wondered how she would contend with missing Bud today; not well, she suspected. On the way from the bus to school, she passed Lacy's and found herself peering into the window as she passed by, imagining that she might see Bud sitting at a table by the window, but all she saw was her own reflection as she slowly walked by.

Francesca was surprised when she saw Bill Adams locking the door of his car. She startled him when she walked up behind him and said, "Hello, Bill." Bill almost jumped, but he had the presence of mind to cover up his surprise quickly, and he greeted her pleasantly.

"Why, hello, Francesca. What brings you to Eton?"

"I'm attending a real estate class. When Florence Evans leaves Benson Real Estate to have her baby, I'm going to take her place."

"Great," Bill said, picking up an overnight bag that sat on the ground beside the car.

"Are you going away?" she asked.

"Yeah, just a short business trip. I'm taking the train. If you don't want to go by boat or bus you have to leave Edgecombe by way of Eton."

"Oh, yes, there's no train into Edgecombe, or planes either."

"No. Edgecombe doesn't want too many interlopers so they keep transportation to a minimum. I'm lucky they let me in." He laughed, then stopped and said, "Good seeing you, Francesca. Give my regards to Amelia and your aunts. I must get to the station and pick up my tickets."

Francesca said good-bye to Bill and continued on her way to her real estate class. She at least had something to tell Amelia. She pondered Bill and his overwhelming shyness where Amelia was concerned. Well, they would have to light a fire under Bill Adams. Francesca made up her mind—she could not have Amelia sitting home night after night longing for Bill to call her. For the life of her, Francesca could not think of any reason why Bill was so uncertain about himself. Why didn't he notice the look in Amelia's eyes when they were together? Things at times were incomprehensible to Francesca; sometimes *everything* was incomprehensible, when it came to Bud.

Chapter Seven

One week went by and Francesca still had not heard any word from Bud. She tried her best not to worry about him, and when Tuesday came she had hoped that she would see Bud at Lacy's, but there had been no sign of him. On Friday her heart was in her mouth as she passed Lacy's, but again there was no sign of Bud and Pike Street hummed with loneliness. So now there was another weekend to get through.

On Saturday morning Charlotte Moore stopped by the house. She was impeccable, as usual; everything about her was just right. Her soft wool dress, of a delicate heather, suited her perfectly and complemented the short natural mink jacket that she wore. Francesca answered the door when Charlotte rang.

"Good morning, Francesca," Charlotte said, taking off her jacket and handing it to Francesca. "Have you heard from any of those young men who were at dinner?"

''I believe Charlie Baxter telephoned, but I wasn't in.''

''Oh, well, he'll call again,'' she said confidently.

''Yes.'' Francesca thought, *I'm afraid he will.* ''I'll call Aunt Lelia and Aunt Daisy,'' she said, going up the steps.

''All right, dear. I'll wait in here,'' Charlotte said, going into the drawing room.

Lelia and Daisy came downstairs together. ''Good morning, Charlotte.'' Lelia gave Charlotte a light kiss on the cheek. Daisy did the same.

''Sit down, Charlotte,'' Lelia said. ''Daisy, would you ask Francesca to get some coffee?''

Daisy obeyed and Francesca came in shortly with the coffee service. She heard Charlotte saying to her aunts, ''You must come with me to Belle Rose. We are going to have to start straightening Keal's affairs out sooner or later. I simply dread going there alone.''

A slight sniffle broke Charlotte's voice. ''Keal would have been thirty soon and, you know, he would have come into his own. As his trustee, I think Fergus has handled all of his holdings very well.'' She touched the corner of her eye with the tip of her handkerchief. ''I don't know why on earth he went out on that boat alone, but the young people of today are so wild and impulsive. He might have been drinking and lost his footing.'' She sighed. ''Who knows?''

Francesca offered Charlotte a cup of coffee, which she accepted without sugar or cream. The serious moment of talk, which Charlotte dominated, seemed to have ended when she turned to Lelia and said, "Charlie Baxter telephoned Francesca, I understand."

"Yes, I believe it was a few days after your dinner party," Lelia replied without very much enthusiasm.

Charlotte then turned her attention to Francesca. "He is from one of Edgecombe's finest families, you know."

"I'm sure he's quite nice." Francesca's evaluation of Charlie was delivered with even less enthusiasm than Lelia's acknowledgement that he had called. "Ruth has some biscuits; I'll get them," she said, and hurried off to the kitchen.

Charlotte's eyes followed Francesca through the door. "She is much too lovely to be sitting home alone. What does she do with her time?" She looked inquiringly at Daisy.

"Well, she has her class in real estate in Eton. She is planning on working with William Benson when Florence leaves," Daisy told her proudly.

"Oh." It was Charlotte's turn to be unimpressed. "There aren't that many eligible young men around." She laughed suddenly. "Heaven only knows, there never have been." She caught the implication of her words and quickly changed the subject. "Do you think that you might be able to go over to Belle Rose on Wednesday?"

"I can't see the hurry. Keal's only been missing a few months, and what about Colin? Shouldn't he be consulted about this?" Daisy asked, not really ready to face the fact that Keal would not be coming back.

"You know, Daisy, as well as I do that Colin English wants as little to do with Edgecombe as possible. He leaves everything to Fergus. Since we were all so close to poor Isabel, I thought you might help with his personal things. Fergus and Axel will handle everything else." She twisted her well-manicured hands in her lap. "It's just out of friendship for Isabel. You both know how much she loved Keal."

"Heaven knows, there should be an end to this." Lelia was near tears in utter frustration. "How does Isabel rest?" She threw her hands up. "Very well, Wednesday is all right with me, if it's all right with Daisy." Lelia submitted to Charlotte in the name of friendship.

The next day Charlotte called and asked if it would be all right to change the day from Wednesday to Tuesday. She had a luncheon to attend that she had forgotten about until she looked at her calendar. Daisy and Lelia were agreeable, so the day was set for Tuesday.

On Tuesday, with a combination of mental and physical stress, Francesca was not feeling well and had awakened with a severe headache. Daisy called her school and told them that Francesca was ill today and would not be in.

"Francesca, do you think you should be left alone?" Daisy asked, bending over the bed.

"I'll be all right, Aunt Daisy. I just don't think that I could manage going in to Eton today."

Daisy felt her forehead. "You don't seem to have

a fever," she said thoughtfully. "We were going to take Ruth with us, but I think she should stay in case you need something."

"Oh, no, Aunt Daisy, I'll be all right. Honest I will. It's just one of those days."

"All right, dear, if you're sure." She started out the door and came back. She took a pen and pad from her purse and wrote something. "If you do need anything, the telephone at Belle Rose is still connected. Just call us there. Perhaps Amelia won't have much to do at work and will come home early."

Daisy was still worried about leaving Francesca alone as she went downstairs where Lelia and Ruth waited. Lelia looked through the stained-glass door. "Ah, there's Jeffers. Come along, Daisy and Ruth." No matter what, Lelia was always the leader. Jeffers was just stepping from the car when he saw the ladies approaching him.

"Good morning, ma'am," Jeffers greeted the women as he opened the back door of the car. Ruth went to the front seat and sat next to Jeffers.

Francesca heard the car pull away. She turned over and tried to go back to sleep, which, after a time, she did. Sometime later on in the morning Francesca came out of her sleep at the sound of a bump from somewhere in the house. She lay quietly for a moment wondering how long she had been asleep. She got out of bed and put her woolen robe on. Pulling the curtains back, she was surprised to find that a gray swirling fog had blanketed Edge-combe, and she could not see the house across the street. Francesca could see the iron gate at the end of the path and tried to make her eyes penetrate the murky mist to see if she saw Charlotte's car at the curb. She then thought that Amelia had probably come back because of the weather, and she went out into the hall and called from the head of the stairs.

"Amelia?" There was no answer. "Amelia?" There was a sound of the door being opened gingerly. There was a surge of fear as her heart began to thump loudly in her ears. "Amelia, is that you?" Francesca got down the steps just in time to hear the faint clank of the iron gate. She rushed to the door and peered out but all she saw was the fog twisting and swirling vacuously about. She pulled the doorknob but the door was locked.

Francesca turned around and went down the hall toward the kitchen. She stopped at the dining room and opened the door. The room was still and serene in the diffused light of the fog. Francesca glanced at the windows and they were undisturbed. She looked puzzled and closed the door and went to the kitchen to check the back door, and it too was locked. Still puzzled, she went to the sink and ran water to make coffee.

Francesca nearly jumped out of her skin when she heard the roar of an automobile's engine race and then stop. At the sound of a key turning in the door, Francesca cowered against the sink, too frightened to move. The door opened and the fog rolled in, wrapped around Amelia.

Amelia entered the house gaily until she saw the expression on Francesca's face.

"Why, Francesca, whatever on earth is the matter?" She went to her and put her hand on Francesca's shoulder.

"I don't know, Amelia. I had the strangest feeling that someone was in the house."

"Oh, nonsense, Francesca. There's nothing in this house worth stealing." Amelia laughed, taking off her coat. "Are you feeling better now?" she asked, taking the coffeepot from her. "Sit down. I'll wash up and make the coffee."

"Thanks, Amelia." Francesca looked up at Amelia when she came back into the kitchen. "What about the toys in the attic? They must be quite valuable. To some antique dealer they might be worth a small fortune."

Running water into the coffeepot, Amelia said, "I doubt that anyone but us even know that they are up there."

Francesca shuddered. "You might think I'm losing my mind, but I have an eerie feeling that there was someone in this house."

"Do you want to call the police?" Amelia asked. The question brought a sobering thought to Francesca, and she looked at Amelia pitifully. "I wouldn't have anything to tell them."

Amelia hugged her and said, "It was probably just the wind."

"Well, for the moment I'm going to have to accept that as the answer."

"What time did Aunt Lelia and Aunt Daisy leave?"

"Oh, I think tennish. I went back to sleep. What time is it now?"

Amelia looked at her watch. "It's almost one o'clock. Why don't I make some lunch for us? I'm sure Aunt Lelia and Aunt Daisy will have lunch with Charlotte." Amelia went to the window and looked out. "You chose a perfect day to be sick. As the saying goes, 'tain't fit for man nor beast out there."

Francesca and Amelia sat down to lunch to one of Amelia's rare successful omelets.

"No news of Bud, I suppose?" Amelia asked kindly.

Francesca shook her head. "It's awful, Amelia, not knowing where he is and not being able to get in touch with him."

"It's a bit odd, you know, Francesca."

"I know. I feel that he might be uncomfortable with us. Everyone knows the Gaylords."

"True. But if there's going to be any kind of relationship, he will have to meet the family. And let's face it, Francesca, that austere facade that our aunts display is mostly because we don't have very much money."

Francesca laughed and said, "So we have to hold our heads a little higher." She was thoughtful. "They're really nice ladies, if Bud would only give them a chance." She stared into her coffee cup. "Do you think that they are happy, not ever having married?"

"They seem to have accepted it," Amelia replied.

"But men and women were meant to be partners in life, and if there isn't someone there to love in that special way, I suppose one is always a little lonely.'' Francesca sighed. ''Amelia, I hope that you and I don't wind up in this house as old ladies sipping tea, just the two of us.''

Amelia snickered. ''I'm afraid that at this moment the odds are not in our favor.'' She saw the sad look that came into Francesca's eyes and said, ''I have the greatest faith that Bud will come back soon. Who knows, he might have been at that place—Lacy's— waiting for you today.''

''No. I knew that he wouldn't be there today, and I simply couldn't face the disappointment.'' Incredulity crossed Francesca's face. ''I can't believe that I forgot to tell you that I saw Bill the other day. He was going into New York on business. I guess *he* at least is back by now.''

This time it was Amelia's turn to be puzzled. ''That was Friday, wasn't it?''

''Why, yes,'' Francesca answered curiously. ''That's funny. I met Fergus in front of Mr. Benson's and he said that Bill was out sick with a touch of flu.''

''Oh, dear. I hope he isn't looking for another job on the q.t.'' Francesca looked worried and Amelia took on a somber tone. The small light that had been in her eyes dimmed as she said, ''The odds of our being spinsters are growing.''

Chapter Eight

Entering the doors of Belle Rose would forever bring a pang of sorrow to the hearts of Lelia and Daisy. They walked resolutely up the path from the driveway through the ever-twisting fog toward the house. Suddenly a colorless form swirled from behind the high shrubbery and floated toward them. Lelia stopped short with Daisy and Ruth piling into her. When the fog melted away from the figure, Lelia saw that it was Cyrus.

"Goodness, man, you nearly scared me to death," she said, catching her breath, more ashamed than annoyed at poor old Cyrus.

"Sorry, Miss Lelia. I heard the car drive up and I didn't know who it might be." The old man's face held the sad look of an old faithful hound dog as he peered at the women through the fog.

"Of course, Cyrus," Lelia said, regaining her dignity. "I gather Miss Charlotte hasn't arrived yet?"

"No, ma'am. No one's here but me."

80

"She will be along soon, I suppose." Lelia gazed off into the fog.

"I can let you in," Cyrus offered.

"That's very good of you, Cyrus. Please do." The four of them walked like disembodied specters as the swirling fog made them formless.

Cyrus opened the door of the great house with its delicate fan lights overhead and the white-trimed Palladian windows staring vacantly over the bay while green ivy climbed up the walls of the house. Cyrus stood aside to let the ladies pass through. For a moment Lelia and Daisy stood silently looking back into the past, when this beautiful house with its magnificent marbled entrance hall and graceful winding staircase rang with laughter echoing through the perfectly designed architecture.

The three women entered the drawing room where a beautiful Peking rug was laid on the hardwood floor, no doubt brought back from China by one of the English sea captains in their trading days with the Orient. An eighteenth-century Italian marble mantel was laid with unlighted logs and an eglomise mirror hung over the cold mantel, flanked by two-armed brass and crystal sconces. Though the room was spacious and elegantly decorated, there was charm and warmth in its well-proportioned walls.

Lelia sat down in one of the comfortable, floral-printed, silk-covered chairs. "We can wait here until Charlotte comes," she said quietly.

Ruth found a chair and sat down. Daisy stood by a fine old Georgian desk. She stared down at a photograph of a smiling Keal English and a group of friends which included Amelia standing near the railing of the *Sea Song*. She picked the photograph up and gazed at it sadly, then with a sigh she slipped it into the drawer of the desk. She closed her eyes for a moment in anguish and silently joined Lelia and Ruth to wait for Charlotte. Shortly they heard the door open and a cold air floated into the room.

''I'm so sorry I wasn't here when you arrived, but I had to wait for the company driver who was off with someone else.'' Charlotte dropped her coat on a nearby chair and looked about the room. ''We've had some very pleasant times in this old house.''

''Yes, we have,'' Daisy assented. ''I wonder when this sad house will see happiness again.''

''It will, I'm sure,'' Charlotte stated, going to the desk. ''Whatever happened to the photograph that was on the desk?''

''I put it into the drawer. At the moment I just can't bear to look at it.

''I understand,'' Charlotte said, turning back to the three women. ''Sally is here with me. So we can get started.''

Friday came and it was again time for hope to rise in Francesca as she took the bus to Eton. In her mind she imagined Bud waiting for her in front of Lacy's, but as she passed by she only saw a few early morning patrons having breakfast.

Francesca barely managed to keep up with her teacher and was only too glad when the class ended. Retracing her steps back along Pike Street where a cold wind was blowing in from the bay, slapping against the green-and-white striped awning of Lacy's Tavern, she knew in her heart that Bud would not be there. There were few people on the street now that the warm Indian summer days had given way to the winter winds. As she neared Lacy's, Francesca saw a tall man emerge through the creaking screen door. He looked as if he might have been a prize-fighter; his muscular arms were bare despite the chill in the air. Even though the man stood in the door-way, Francesca was determined to steal a quick glance through the window. When she was directly in front of Lacy's, she looked quickly into the win-dow, which was to no avail because she only saw her own reflection staring back at her. As she passed the big man, he looked at her searchingly; a few feet past him, she heard her name called.

"Miss Mayhew?"

Francesca turned in surprise. "Yes?"

"You are Miss Francesca Mayhew?" he asked, walking up to her. He wore an apron of heavy white cotton tied with the bib tucked down around his waist. He stopped and put his big hands on his hips.

"I've been running in and out of that door all morning, afraid I'd miss you." Extending a big hand to Francesca, he said, "I'm Tom Lacy."

Francesca accepted the offered hand. "How do you do, Mr. Lacy?"

"I have a message for you," he said, smiling with perfect even white teeth in his masculine, good-looking face. Francesca's eyes were filled with cu-riosity as she looked into the dark eyes of Tom Lacy.

"Bud telephoned the bar this morning and asked

me to tell you that he will be a little longer than he had planned.'' Lacy smiled again. ''But he will be back as soon as he can.'' He was thoughtful for a moment. ''He said to tell you not to worry.''

Francesca had to restrain herself from throwing her arms around Tom Lacy's neck and giving him a big kiss. She was so filled with happiness that she felt like champagne bubbles, and all she could say was, ''Thank you so much, Mr. Lacy. Thank you so much. You are very kind.''

''Not at all, Miss Mayhew, it was my pleasure. Would you like to come in and have a cup of coffee?''

''Thank you very much, but I must catch my bus back to Edgecombe.''

''Some other time, then,'' Tom Lacy said, backing away to return to the warmth of the restaurant.

''Yes, thank you very much.'' She hurried off to the bus station to catch the 3:30 bus. She offered her hand in farewell to Lacy.

Francesca was so happy at hearing some news of Bud that when she alighted from the bus she immediately went to a public telephone and called Amelia at the real estate office. When Amelia heard the news, she asked Francesca to meet her at Mr. Benson's and ride with her to pick up their aunts at Belle Rose.

''You can have a good look inside. They're still sorting out Keal's things, which is very unpleasant for them.'' Francesca heard the compassion in the silence that followed Amelia's voice over the wire.

"I'll walk over and be there in a few minutes. Good-bye, Amelia."

Francesca hung the receiver back into its hook and started for the office of Mr. Benson, who was not there when she arrived.

"Hello, Amelia," she said, closing the door behind her. "Was I true to my word?"

"Yes," Amelia said, looking at her watch. "I'll get my things and we can pick the aunties up. I'm sure they're dying to get home. I don't know why Charlotte's putting them through this, but they did love Keal, so I guess it's only fitting that they should take charge since he has no close family nearby."

The house was approached from a rear driveway that was nestled between giant rhododendrons. The little foreign car took every bump on the driveway as Amelia held the steering wheel in a firm grip, which made driving the car look as if it was hard work, bringing to Francesca's mind that she would probably look into a small American car. The car heaved and bumped along the road until they came to the clearing where the weathered fence stood barrier to the footpath that led down to the *Sea Song* quietly bobbing on the water.

"Oh, stop for a moment," Francesca asked Amelia. "Isn't she beautiful?"

"Yes. I wonder what they will do with the *Sea Song?* Poor, poor boat."

Amelia started the engine up again and they rode the rest of the way to the house without speaking.

The rear of Belle Rose was sheltered by tall trees

and brick garden walls covered with ivy, but the whole front of the house faced the open bay.

Francesca stepped from the car and surveyed the beautiful structure. "It's lovely."

"Come on, wait until you've seen the inside." Amelia led her along the path where she had been so intimidated by Cyrus. Amelia opened the door and called, "Yoo-hoo, Aunt Lelia? Aunt Daisy? We're here." There was no answer and Amelia went to the foot of the winding stairs and looked up, calling, "Aunt . . ." She stopped when Lelia's head appeared over the railing.

"Hello, Aunt Lelia. Francesca's here with me."

"We're just about finished. We'll be down in a moment." She disappeared from the railing, but suddenly reappeared. "Show Francesca around the house." She vanished again.

"Come on, let me show you the sitting room." Amelia smiled. "The grand tour."

Francesca was in awe of everything that she saw. "It's even more beautiful than I dreamed," she said. "Did you know Keal English very well?"

"Oh, yes. We grew up together because of the closeness of Isabel. We saw a lot of each other through the years. I miss him very much."

"I'm sorry, Amelia."

When they finished looking around downstairs, Amelia took Francesca up the sweeping stairs. She showed her the spacious bedrooms with their variety of mantels, some were beautifully carved wood and some were different shades of marble. Most of the rooms looked out over the bay, which was gray today. Had there been sunlight, they would have been flooded in brilliant light, but instead, today the rooms were cast in a pearl-gray glow. Most of the floors were covered in old Oriental carpeting with rich silk drapes at the windows.

"Oh, Amelia, all of this and most of the family is dead," Francesca said with pity.

"It is sad, isn't it?"

"Come, Amelia and Francesca, we're ready to leave."

"Hello, Aunt Lelia, Aunt Daisy," Francesca greeted her aunts, whom she had not yet seen.

"What happened to Charlotte?" Francesca asked as they went back into the drawing room.

"She had to meet Fergus," Daisy answered.

"What a lovely old Georgian desk," Francesca said, feeling the satiny texture of the fine wood.

"Yes, it is," Lelia replied, looking at the desk with an appreciation of its quality. "Come, girls, Daisy and I are anxious to get home." She gazed around the room. "Away from this house of sadness."

Ruth met them at the door and helped Lelia and Daisy with their coats. "Dinner is ready whenever you want to eat," she announced, going back to the kitchen.

"Funny," Lelia said, glancing around the entrance hall. She sniffed a bit.

"Funny? What seems to be funny?" Daisy asked.

"I don't know, I just had a strange feeling. I don't know what it was." She gave an airy wave of her hand and said, "Silly," dismissing whatever feeling that had come over her. What she did not want to say was that she thought she smelled Isabel's scent, Chanel Number 5.

Lelia announced one morning that they were going to have some people in to dinner. She had just realized that Francesca had been home over a month, the holidays would soon roll around, and they had had no one in to welcome her home.

"Come into the sitting room," she told Francesca and Amelia, carrying a list in her hand. "I have a list of people that I'm asking to dinner. Now, I want to know whom you two young ladies would like to ask." She walked ahead reading the list.

Francesca gave Amelia a quick glance and said, "What about Bill Adams?"

Lelia eyed Amelia with a comprehending look. "Yes, that would be nice." Amelia swallowed hard. Francesca smiled knowingly at her.

"All right. Now who else?" Francesca wished that she could have invited Bud, but she had no idea where he was and she doubted that he would have come anyway. She shrugged her shoulders at Amelia when her aunt wasn't looking.

"What about Charlie Baxter?"

Lelia looked at her as if she thought she had made a mistake, but then said, "All right, Charlie," and dotted his name with a snort.

"Well, that's that. There's Ophelia and Robert and, of course, Charlotte and Fergus." Lelia tapped her cheek with the pen as she thought of whom else to add to the list. "Oh, I think I'll ask Axel. He's always a charming, charming man." Lelia wrote his

name down. "Axel and Nora. I'd better ask Josephine LaSalle. I don't want this list to get out of
hand, so I'd better stop this moment. No adding any
more people to the list." Lelia got up and left the
room. "If you think of anyone else, we might be
able to squeeze one or two more in." She left the
room with a cheerful gait.

When Lelia was out of hearing distance, Amelia
leaned over and asked, "Do you really want that
awful snob Charlie Baxter to come?"

"He was the only one I could think of, and it
really doesn't make any difference who my dinner
partner is. If it can't be Bud, then it doesn't matter
who it is." Francesca smiled. "But isn't it nice that
Bill is being invited?"

"Yes, that was thoughtful of you. Thanks,
Francesca."

"What are families for?" She grinned broadly,
her walnut eyes dancing impishly. "Do you know,
Amelia, I think that one day we will have nice lives.
You will have Bill and I will have Bud." Francesca
stretched out on the sofa and clasped her hands behind her head, her thick hair flowing through her
fingers. "It must be, Amelia." The news of Bud was
now beginning to fade back into the realm of uncertainty. For a few days it was enough to give her
enormous hope that Bud would soon return, but
there would have to be more before she could gain
any confidence in their rather odd relationship.

Amelia spoke to Francesca candidly. "You do
know, Francesca, that if he doesn't start to behave
properly . . . and I don't mean his longshoreman

manners; they probably are as good as any." Amelia frowned as a thought occurred to her. "You don't think he's hiding a wife and children someplace, do you?"

Francesca turned and looked at Amelia, fear in her clear brown eyes that only a few moments ago looked so happy. "Amelia, I never thought of that." She suddenly looked sick. "You have really given me something to worry about."

Amelia saw the terrible disturbed look on Francesca's face and tried to retract her words. "Oh, I was just thinking out loud and it's a ridiculous idea. Please forget that I said it."

Francesca said weakly, "It is a thought, isn't it?"

Lelia and Daisy's dinner party was on Friday night. Francesca had attended her class and come home without word of Bud. She had not even seen Tom Lacy, and if he had had any news of Bud, she was quite certain that he would have awaited her outside the restaurant as before. So Francesca's spirits were not at their highest as she helped with the preparations for the dinner.

When everything was in readiness, the women went to their rooms to dress. The guests were due to arrive at 8:00 and Francesca dressed in a soft silk shirt of pale yellow and a long dirndl Indian silk skirt with a print of yellow and black. She pulled on black sandals and sat in an ungraceful pose on the side of her bed. She was dressed and ready at 7:30.

She got up, appraised herself in the mirror, walking around the room a bit, and with nothing more to do, she went into the hallway. No one else seemed to be ready, so she opened the attic door and decided to visit the toys again.

The overhead light did not go on, so she felt her way to the small lamp that sat in the corner next to the wealth of toys. Francesca turned the lamp on and was surprised to find how little light it gave off. She sat huddled in the corner on what was probably a century-old child's chair. She picked up one of the incredibly beautiful china dolls. Francesca looked into the blue glass eyes and tried to imagine the joy of the first little girl who held her, and leaned back in the little chair looking like Alice in Wonderland.

Allowing herself a moment to indulge in self-pity, Francesca closed her eyes and let the tears swim. She opened them quickly and whipped away the tears before they fell as she heard the attic door creak open. She started to stand and call to Amelia when she heard the whispering voices of a man and a woman. The woman said, ''It has to be here.'' The masculine voice whispered back, ''This is a crazy time to look.''

Francesca stood up, bumping against one of the toys, sending it to the floor with a thud. She heard the door quickly shut and she was left in silence. *Who on earth was that, and what are they looking for?* Francesca had to reason with herself that she had actually heard the voices. The idea of someone in search of some secret quest in her aunts' house was unimaginable.

The thought flashed across Francesca's mind that it might have something to do with her. After all, her father was an ambassador of the United States and privileged to many secrets, both of national and international importance, and he had certainly dealt with agents of all kinds, but any fool would know that she would have absolutely no knowledge of what the U.S. government, or any other governments, had in mind.

Switching the lamp off, Francesca hurriedly lifted the hem of her skirt and made her way through the dark room as fast as she could without killing herself. Her first thought was to find Amelia. She knocked quickly on Amelia's door and let herself in without waiting for an invitation.

''Amelia!'' she called before she saw that the room was empty. She closed the door quickly and ran down the steps. She opened the door to the drawing room and found that most of the guests had arrived. Dr. Defoe stood at the mantel with Charlotte, who looked stunning in a sapphire gown.

Charlie Baxter rose from a chair in the corner of the room when Francesca entered, his eyes beaming. Axel stood chatting with Amelia, amused by something that she had said. Lelia sat with a man whom Francesca did not know, and Daisy stood with a woman that Francesca assumed was Josephine LaSalle.

The man sitting with Lelia was introduced as Seth Anderson, and the man who stood with Daisy and Josephine was Walter Skinner, from another one of Edgecombe's old families. Francesca did not see Ophelia in the room and Bill Adams had come up behind her as she secretly surveyed the room from the doorway. Amelia excused herself from Axel and went to Francesca.

"Where were you?" she whispered discreetly.

"In the attic."

"In the attic! Whatever for?" Amelia asked.

"I'll tell you later, when we go in to help Ruth with the hors d'oeuvres."

Amelia was worried as she gazed uncertainly at Francesca, more for her mental state than for anything sinister afoot. Francesca went to Daisy and asked, "Would you like Amelia and me to go in now and help Ruth?"

"Yes, dear, that would be nice." Daisy smiled benevolently at her niece.

Francesca caught Amelia by the arm and said, "Come on."

Amelia went with her in what Amelia thought was a highly agitated state, which was unusual for Francesca. When they entered the kitchen, Ruth was just leaving with a tray of stuffed mushrooms. Francesca held the door for her and then practically dragged Amelia through it.

"Amelia," she started breathlessly, "I was sitting in the attic in the corner where the toys are." She added, "Feeling sorry for myself, when I heard the door open. I thought it was you, so I stood up, knocking over a wooden toy. I started to call you to let you know where I was when I heard two voices whispering, a man and a woman. I couldn't make out who they were, but they said something strange."

Francesca repeated the words. " 'It has to be

here,' and the man whispered 'This is a crazy time to look.' That's when I knocked over the toy and they quickly shut the door and left.'' Francesca looked at Amelia. ''You see, someone was here on Tuesday. I don't know how they got in, but someone is looking for something in this house.''

''But what, Francesca?'' Amelia's face wore an expression of disbelief.

''I don't know. I thought you might have some idea of what Aunt Lelia and Aunt Daisy might have that is valuable to someone.'' Amelia only looked blank. ''Let's not tell Aunt Daisy and Aunt Lelia yet. There's no need to worry them just now,'' Francesca said.

Ruth came back into the kitchen, cutting off their conversation abruptly. Amelia ended it with a quiet, ''All right.'' They both took a tray filled with little tidbits of meat and fish and entered the drawing room. Francesca caught sight of Fergus talking happily to Ophelia, and Francesca remembered that they had not been in the room when she came downstairs.

Fergus greeted Francesca and Amelia with, ''Ah, there are my two lovely girls,'' as he reached for a small open sandwich of salmon.

Francesca and Amelia moved around the room offering the contents of their trays; every once in a while they stole a glance at each other. When they took their trays back to the kitchen, Francesca asked Amelia, ''When did Fergus arrive?''

Amelia thought for a moment. ''He wasn't there when we came into the kitchen.''

''What about Ophelia?''

"She came in with Dr. Defoe. She had gone to the powder room. You don't think it was Fergus and Ophelia?" Amelia looked at Francesca skeptically.

"I don't know." Worry with a hint of fear filled Francesca's eyes. "I'm afraid." She smiled. "I who have grown up in the midst of intrigue. This is no doubt insignificant compared to what goes on in government."

Francesca's eyes became distant and she said, "But that was never personal. No one ever came into our home."

Chapter Nine

Thanksgiving had come and gone, which meant that Christmas was just around the corner. Edgecombe was lighted with the festivity of the season. Everywhere bright lights twinkled in shop windows that were filled with all sorts of delightful things. Boxes wrapped in gaily colored papers and tied with silver and gold ribbon sat under shining tinsel strung through green garlands of pine dotted with red holly berries.

The air was filled with the sound of church bells chiming Christmas carols; this made even Francesca feel good. She took her last bus to Eton before the holidays. Eton was also dressed for the Christmas holidays with lights and garlands strung overhead across the street from the lamp posts, and Santa Clauses stood on street corners ringing brass bells next to big black kettles, while soldiers of the Salvation Army blew big brass horns.

Francesca passed by Lacy's on the way to her class and she noticed that Lacy's too had spared nothing in its greeting to Christmas as gay wreaths with large red ribbons hung in the windows with small electric candles burning in the center. The sight of Lacy's brought a stab of pain to Francesca's heart as she thought of Bud and how it would have been had he been there, instead of who knows where.

Today would be the last class for a while. No classes meant no hope of seeing Bud at all. Francesa's heart was beginning to sink even with all the colorful lights and the cheerful mood of all the holiday shoppers that she passed on the streets.

Francesca's class had a small Christmas party. All students joyfully wished one another a Merry Christmas as they parted. One young man looked up at the sky as the first snowflake fell. He smiled and said, "It's beginning to look a lot like Christmas," as many more fluffy snowflakes filled the air. Everyone laughed gaily and waved good-bye.

Francesca started her lonely walk up Pike Street to her bus. The snow was falling heavily now, collecting in corners and covering tops of cars. It was so heavy now that Francesca found it difficult to see. She was nearing Lacy's and she saw the glow of the electric candles from the windows giving a yellow cast to the new snow. The shadow of a man stood waiting under the green awning that was too laden with snow to flap in the wind.

As she drew near, the figure of the man left the protection of the awning and walked toward Francesca, and suddenly it was as if the sun had burst forth and bluebirds joined in harmony with the nightingales in song and all was right with heaven. She stopped short and said, "Oh, Bud," and tears of joy filled her eyes as she rushed into his waiting arms. Francesca had not wanted to cry, but she could not stop the tears as Bud kissed her and held her close to him, to the extreme pleasure of passersby.

"Come inside," Bud said, leading her into Lacy's.

A giant fir tree stood in one corner blinking with red and green lights; shining balls of yellow, green, and red dangled from dark braches with garlands of silver and gold draped from the top with an angel at the very tip. Tom Lacy would never have dreamed of having an artificial tree in his tavern.

"Sit here," Bud directed Francesca. They sat down next to the window where they could watch the snow fall.

Bud took Francesca's hands across the table and kissed her fingertips.

"I was so afraid, Bud. I thought that I would never see you again."

"You will always see me again, Francesca. One day I'll remind you of this moment."

Francesca smiled shyly and said, "Is that a promise?"

"That's a fact." He did not smile. It was as if a wind had come and suddenly blown away his light heart.

He noticed the questioning gaze in Francesca's eyes and as suddenly as his cheerfulness had disappeared, it returned again.

"Will you stay for a while?" she asked hopefully.

"I can't promise that just yet . . ." He saw the disappointment in her eyes. "But I will promise to be with you on Christmas day."

"You will come to dinner, then." Her face was aglow.

"No, I can't do that, but I will meet you after dinner, if that's all right."

"Well, I suppose I can get away, but you do know that this will probably not sit very well with my aunts. They will want to know why you won't come to the house." Francesca twisted her hands. "And that sort of thing."

"I will come to the house, very soon."

Francesca decided to be frank and ask Bud if he was shy about meeting her aunts, and she, so to speak, took the bull by the horn.

"Bud," she started hesitantly, "are you uncomfortable about meeting my aunts . . . well, because you are a longshoreman?"

A twinkle lit his eyes for a moment before he replied, "Sort of."

"But can't you see that this is a new age? People don't care where other people are from now, or what kind of work they do. It doesn't matter to me." Francesca was near tears.

Bud smiled at her and said, "I'm glad that you feel that way."

Francesca sniffed a bit and returned Bud's smile. "You know, my aunts are very proud and seem unapproachable, old family and that sort of thing, but half of it is because we have very little else other than pride."

Bud reached across the table and took Francesca's soft hands in his hard, callused ones and spoke softly to her. "You are a very understanding and beautiful woman, Francesca. I am deeply touched by what you have said, and I love you very much."

Tears swam in Francesca's eyes and she said, "I love you very, very much."

"And even though I can't come to Christmas dinner, it will still be a happy Christmas." He tilted her chin, forcing her to raise her eyes and look into his. "Just knowing how much we love each other will sustain us for this Christmas." There was a strong glint in his blue eyes.

"It will have to," Francesca said resolutely.

"You do believe me, don't you?"

"Yes, I believe you." She forced herself to smile at him.

"Good. Now what about some lunch?"

"I'm to happy to eat anything."

"Well, Tom can't run a tavern for happy people. So let's have a little something, shall we?" He picked up the menu, scanning the offerings.

"Where will you have Christmas dinner?" she asked.

"Tom Lacy has asked me to have dinner with him and his family."

"Oh." Francesca was a little hurt and she masked it by not making any further remarks about Christmas dinner. "Mr. Lacy seems like a very nice man."

"He's a good friend."

*   *   *

Murmuring snow fell gently over Edgecombe, making it even more tidy in the blue and white light of evening. Francesca pulled her hat further down over her head and though the snow pulled her feet down, she hardly noticed as her spirits soared as high as they could go without touching heaven. She paused and looked at the Christmas trees that were piled against a lamp post and she thought, *We must get a tree.* She found a phone booth on the corner of the street and went in to call Amelia.

She heard the phone on the other end ring. It rang and rang and just as she was about to hang up, she heard Amelia answer breathlessly.

"Hello, Amelia. I was just about to hang up."

"Sorry, I was just going out the door."

"Do you think we could pick up a Christmas tree before we go home?"

"Good idea. Where are you?"

"I'm on the corner of Holt and Bragg Streets." Francesca blinked as a snowflake fell into her eye.

"Wait for me. I'll be there in a few minutes."

Francesca busied herself with choosing the most beautiful trees to show Amelia when she arrived, which was only minutes later. But before she arrived, Francesca had telephoned her aunts and asked if they might invite Bill Adams for Christmas dinner. Daisy was very agreeable, so when Amelia arrived Francesca had two pieces of good news to tell her.

Amelia was almost as elated as Francesca over the news of Bud, but she reminded Francesca that Bill would have to be asked first and then accept.

"But we can do that when we get home," Francesca said gleefully as they chose a tall fir tree that was picture-perfect.

''Who's going to ask Bill?'' Amelia asked.

''Why, you are, of course,'' Francesca answered with a ''what a silly question'' tone of voice.

''I don't think I have the nerve.'' They argued the question all the way to Holly Street and as they took the tree off the top of the car.

''Well, let Aunt Lelia ask him.''

''Oh, fine, Miss Courageous.'' Amelia laughed.

Lelia did ask Bill and he was very grateful, but he was going home to Boston for the holidays.

''Well, it looks as if it will be just the family for Christmas,'' Amelia said with disappointment edging her voice. But the next day Bill called Amelia at the office and asked her if she would have dinner with him when he returned on the twenty-eighth. Agape, Amelia could barely get out a yes, and it was her turn to float on heavenly pink clouds.

Amelia and Francesca brought the Christmas tree decorations down from the attic and the four women, two generations apart, enjoyed the age-old tradition of trimming the Christmas tree with brightly colored balls and silver and gold horns with festoons of silver garlands draped around the full and fragrant branches. Some of the ornaments had been in the Gaylord family as long as Daisy and Lelia could remember.

When they finished they turned the lamps off and turned on the tiny white tree lights.

''It's beautiful.'' Lelia sighed.

"I think the tree becomes more beautiful each year," Daisy agreed, enraptured.

Amelia brought in coffee and Francesca put Leontyne Price's Christmas album on the stereo. The women sat in the drawing room watching the twinkling bright lights going on and off while the fire in the grate sparkled and crackled, mingling the aroma of burning wood with the fragrance of the fir tree. Francesca sat quietly listening to the merry sounds of Christmas. Daisy sighed and spoke reverently as Leontyne Price sang "Ave Maria." "Surely her voice is next to those of the angels."

"It is lovely." It seemed to be a time for sighing, and Francesca drew in a breath.

Later in the evening after everyone had retired to their rooms, Francesca sat on the corner of her bed and said, "I'm all right, Mother and Daddy. I am, really." And she knew that she would have to let the bitter tears out for a few minutes. This was the first Christmas in her life that she had not been in the loving company of her parents. Even when the time schedule had been close, her father had always made it home for Christmas.

Francesca remembered how she would wait at the window watching until she saw her father come up the path, and how excitedly she would call to her mother to "Come quickly—Daddy's home!" When her sobbing had ceased Francesca went to the window and sat on the sill watching the softly falling snow. Perhaps now only the good memories were starting to come.

Chapter Ten

On Christmas Eve Francesca had completed her shopping and in the quiet of her room sat on the floor wrapping gifts. She had gotten a lovely white lace blouse for Lelia with a high ruffled collar and a bottle of her favorite perfume. For Daisy she had found an old set of *Anthology of the World's Greatest Poems*, selected by the great poet Edwin Markham, and a beautiful leather-bound biography of Lord Byron. For Amelia, Francesca had a strand of pearls that she had bought on a trip to Japan with her parents. She held the pearls up and admired their luster. She had seen Amelia's imitation strand which did not look bad but she was sure that Amelia would like these. Francesca now had her mother's flawless strand that glowed with the luminous light of the moon. And for Bud, she had chosen very carefully a beautiful navy blue silk scarf with a paisley print similar to the tie that he had worn on their first official date.

Francesca wrapped it in a red metallic paper and

finished it with a green satin ribbon with a fluffy bow. Immersed in the spirit of Christmas, its warmth and love, one always found a moment to remember those who were no longer here, and Keal English came to Francesca's mind. She felt pity for his father who had lost his son, and for Bill Adams who had lost his good friend.

Gifts were exchanged and delighted in. Christmas dinner over, a comfortable quiet settled over the house. A fire burned warmly in the fireplace while the lights danced on the tree. Francesca, in a quiet peace of mind but filled with great expectation, asked Amelia, who was wearing her gift from Francesca, "Do you think it will be all right to leave soon?"

"I don't see why not. The aunties have gone up-stairs and I'm going to spend the rest of the evening looking in the mirror at my pearls," Amelia said, fondling the strand.

"You nut!" Francesca laughed, pleased that her gift was so well liked.

"Look, I'll drop you downtown and come right back. That way I won't cause Bud any discomfort. Get your coat."

"Okay. I'll tell Aunt Lelia and Aunt Daisy that I'm going to meet a friend for a little while."

Francesca was back in a few minutes with her coat and Bud's gift.

Amelia dropped Francesca near the bus station with a warning that this relationship would have to have a resolution soon. The streets were quiet, with most people home with their families seeing the end of Christmas Day together. Francesca walked across the street to the bus station to wait for Bud, who drove up in a few minutes, this time in a Chrysler sedan. He parked in the shadows and called to Francesca, who had expected to see the red car. He pushed her door open and she got in.

"Hello, darling," he said, leaning over to kiss her. "Merry Christmas."

"Merry Christmas," Francesca replied, handing Bud his gift.

Bud accepted the box with some shame. Awkwardly he took the scarf from its wrapping and put it around his neck. "Thank you very much." He gazed at Francesca in the semidarkness. "It's very nice. How does it look?"

Francesca playfully appraised him and said, "Very handsome." Bud looked embarrassed and said, "I have a present for you, but it will take a while for me to get it." He smiled at her. "In fact I have two presents for you." His eyes became serious. "Will you wait just a little while longer?"

Francesca smiled at him. "It sounds very promising."

"It is. Now that I'm cozy and warm in my new scarf, let's go someplace and have a Christmas drink to the future."

They drove to a pub near the docks of Eton that had the decor of a ship. There were fishing nets strung from the ceiling with corks pitted throughout; big gray barrels filled with peanuts ringed the room. Ship lanterns lit with candles lighted the room, showing weathered paneling and green wreaths hanging at paned windows.

They were seated at a table in a cozy corner, the light of the candles softening any doubts or worries that might have been on their faces. When their drinks came, Bud sat silently twisting his brandy glass around on the table. After a while he said, "I think that I will soon have my affairs straightened out and we will be able to have a normal relationship." He stopped and smiled. "I'll come to your house and meet your family." He stared beseechingly into her eyes. "I promise I will do everything that you ask, soon," he added.

"Everything, Bud?" Francesca laughed and squinted her eyes at him. "I'll have you in my power."

He took her hands again. "You already have me in your power."

Francesca made light of the situation and said, "I won't be too hard on you."

Bud laughed and wiped away imaginary sweat. "That's a relief."

Bud returned Francesca to Holly Street and watched her walk safely through the door. She did not know that again she would go for weeks without hearing a word from him.

For the next few days Amelia walked on air, preparing for her date with Bill. When the magic moment arrived, Amelia was beside herself with anxiety as Francesca helped her dress in the yellow angora sweater that Francesca had given her. They both scrutinized the soft white wool skirt that Amelia was wearing with the sweater. Amelia was very pleased when she draped her treasured pearls around her neck. She peered into the mirror.

"Oh, Francesca, do you think I have on too much blush?"

"No. It's just enough," Francesca assured Amelia, smiling at her in the looking-glass. Lelia came into the room, overhearing Amelia's words of self-doubt, and said with a tender edge to her voice, "Why, Amelia, you look just fine, and I'm sure Bill will be very pleased. You are, after all, a . . ."

Amelia turned to look at her aunt. Lelia swallowed and finished her statement. "A lovely young lady." Amelia looked puzzled as she watched her aunt leave the room. Francesca too was puzzled; she had also thought that Lelia was about to say something else before she caught herself.

The sound of the doorbell ringing downstairs sent Amelia into a state of fluttering. "It's Bill!"

"I'll answer the door and you can make a grand entrance." Francesca smiled, closing the door behind her.

Francesca let Bill in, who seemed almost as much in a siege of nerves as Amelia.

"Hello, Francesca," he said, taking off his camel-hair coat and giving it to her.

"Hello, Bill. Amelia will be down in a few minutes. Come into the sitting room and I'll get you a drink." Francesca showed Bill in. "Aunt Lelia and Aunt Daisy will want to say hello. I'll tell them that you are here."

Francesca returned with Lelia and Daisy, who were genuinely pleased to see Bill.

''Ruth will bring in some sherry while we wait for Amelia.'' Lelia aimlessly pointed out a chair to Bill. ''Please have a seat, Bill.''

''Thank you, ma'am.'' Bill sat down nervously.

Ruth brought the sherry in, in the finest crystal decanter with lovely cut crystal sherry glasses on a well-polished silver tray. Francesca was beginning to have some insight into her aunts and she knew that this bit of graciousness was because they approved of Bill. She wondered what Bud's sherry would be served from, if he ever came to the house. Francesca added to her thoughts as she listened to the small talk that the three were indulging in.

Amelia came into the room. A cool glow like the light of the rainbow had settled over her. She carried her coat over her arm. Bill rose from his seat, his eyes fixed on Amelia in awe as he took her coat and helped her on with it. Amelia accepted his help as if her heart had never in its life skipped a beat. Bill thanked Lelia and Daisy as all three women went to the door with him and Amelia. When the door shut behind them, Francesca stood and watched them walk down the steps on a cloud, their feet nowhere near the earth's floor. There were only the two of them, the tails of their coats flapping in the wind as Amelia looked up into Bill's face.

Oh, Bud, she thought, *this is how it's supposed to be.* Francesca felt a sob in her throat as she went up the steps to her room with dragging feet that were weighted down in doubt.

Daisy met her at the top of the stairs and spoke kindly.

"He's a nice young man."

"I think so, too, and I'm glad that you like him, because Amelia likes him so much."

Daisy chuckled. "I think he likes Amelia quite a bit, too." She gazed fondly at Francesca. "You too will meet some nice young man soon. I'm afraid it's getting on to the time that our darling girls will be leaving us."

Francesca put her arms around her. "You will never get rid of us. I can promise you that."

"Well, I hope that you won't go too far away." Daisy gave Francesca a tight hug around the shoulders.

"Never." Francesca kissed Daisy on her round cheek.

Leaving her aunt at her bedroom door, Francesca said, "I promise not to wait up for Amelia if you won't."

Daisy laughed. "I promise, but you had better speak to Lelia."

Francesca laughed with Daisy. "Good night, Aunt Daisy. Sleep well." Francesca knew that they would all stay awake until Amelia came in, but she would be the only one who would go to Amelia's room for a report on how the evening had gone; she was almost as excited as Amelia.

Francesca did not sleep a wink until Amelia came home. She crept down the hall and sat on Amelia's bed while she undressed and together they assessed the evening, which Amelia could only describe as "heavenly."

Things started to go well with Amelia and Bill after their first date. Bill called regularly and the bond that binds two souls was strengthening by the day.

Francesca's real estate classes were winding down, and soon she would have her license as a bona fide real estate saleswoman, and with no excuses whatsoever to go into Eton and no hope of seeing Bud.

After her Tuesday class, Francesca met Amelia in her office and drove with her to pick Lelia and Daisy up. They were going regularly to Belle Rose, putting into order what they could of Keal English's belongings.

Francesca thought that if she went to Belle Rose every day of her life she would never stop being in awe of the beauty of the house.

"Hello, Cyrus," Amelia called to the old man who lurked behind a hedge. He did not seem eager to be seen and not particularly interested in greeting the two young women. Francesca waved to Cyrus, who acknowledged their greetings with a muttered "Afternoon," and stood silently watching Francesca and Amelia until they disappeared into the house.

They found Daisy sitting in one of the elegant wing-back chairs before a brightly burning fire that could have been called cheerful had the circumstances been different.

Francesca peered at Daisy with a measure of concern. "Aunt Daisy, are you feeling all right?" she asked.

Daisy tried to rouse herself with a cheerful smile. She had not heard Amelia and Francesca come in and tried to make the pretense of well-being, dismissing their concern. "Oh, I'm all right, just a little tired."

"Have you had lunch?" Francesca asked as Amelia stood by with a concerned frown between her dark eyes.

"I'll get Aunt Lelia. I think we should get you home," Amelia said worriedly to Daisy and immediately left the room in search of Lelia.

"We had lunch with Charlotte." Daisy got around to answering Francesca's question.

Lelia came into the room with Charlotte close behind her. "You don't look well, Daisy." She felt her sister's forehead. "You don't have any fever. Do you think the seafood might have disagreed with you?" Lelia's words were matter-of-fact, but worry blanketed her face.

"Come, Daisy, darling, let us help you to the car." Charlotte took Daisy under the arm and tried to raise her up, almost toppling under Daisy's weight. Francesca took Daisy's other arm and together they got Daisy on her feet.

"There. I feel better already," she said.

"Regardless, we're going to take you home now," Charlotte stated firmly. "We can finish this another time."

When they entered the hall, with Daisy bundled up against the chill, Lelia looked around curiously and delicately sniffed the air. ''Who's wearing Chanel?''

They all looked at one another, puzzled, and each said, ''Not I.''

''Odd,'' Lelia said as they walked out of Belle Rose to Amelia's car.

Daisy was put to bed against her protests of being only a little tired.

The next morning she remained in bed and Francesca went to Belle Rose with Lelia and Charlotte. Charlotte's chauffeur picked them up and as Francesca was leaving, Amelia whispered to her that she was having lunch with Bill.

''Ah-ha.'' Francesca laughed softly, leaving Amelia smiling like the cat who had swallowed the canary.

As Jeffers held the door for them to alight from the car, Francesca saw old Cyrus bending over some shrubs. She saw his eyes raise secretively as they passed him. It was quite evident that he was going to pretend not to see them, so Francesca decided to let him have his way.

Inside Belle Rose, the three women shed their coats and hung them in the closet. A woman in a black-and-white maid's uniform came through the dining room door.

''Good morning, Mrs. Moore. Good morning, Miss Gaylord.'' The woman nodded to Francesca and Charlotte introduced them.

''I'm glad that you could come, Bessie.'' Charlotte gratefully patted Bessie on the arm. ''Go through all the closets and pack the things in the boxes that Jeffers is bringing in.'' Charlotte looked at her watch. ''We will work until noon and then have some lunch. Sally's made a very good soup.'' She sighed. ''Then I think we should call it a day.''

Readying themselves for the task of clearing away the accumulation of a young life, Francesca ventured to ask what would happen to an old life. ''What is going to happen to Cyrus? He seems so lost.''

Charlotte took a deep breath. ''I suppose we can find a retirement home for him. I don't think that he will be able to find employment anywhere.''

''What a pity,'' Francesca whispered remorsefully. ''And Belle Rose?''

Charlotte's head twisted a bit and her chin lifted. ''I don't really know. I would hate to see strangers come into this house or into Lyre Hall, for that matter.'' She studied her hands for a moment and repeated, ''I really don't know.''

Francesca helped as long as she was needed, then she took a walk around the grounds of Belle Rose. She saw Cyrus and went over to speak to him.

''Hello, Cyrus. My, you keep the garden beautifully.'' A flicker of pride escaped from behind the eyes that viewed Francesca with subdued interest.

''Good morning, Miss.'' He surveyed his work without acknowledging Francesca's compliment.

''I thought I would take a walk around the grounds while my aunt and Mrs. Moore rest a bit, and have something to eat.'' Cyrus spread a hand out and said, ''Help yourself, Miss.'' Francesca walked away knowing that she had not made a friend, saying, ''Thank you,'' over her shoulder.

Aimlessly wandering along she came upon a long
garage that was large enough to hold eight cars. She
opened the door and saw four cars—a dark green
Rolls Royce, an expensive-looking sports car, a station wagon, and a long dark blue limousine.

Francesca guessed that the sports car had been the
favorite. She peered into the luxurious Rolls with its
cream-colored leather upholstery, and marveled at
the sports car which was an old SS 100 Jaguar. Francesca knew nothing about cars but this one looked
like a prize.

Her footsteps resounded hollowly against the cold
concrete as she walked back to the door and backed
out, pulling the door shut. She jumped when a voice
behind her said, "Doing a bit of exploring, Miss
Mayhew?" The voice spoke with amusement. She
turned to see Axel Kingsly smiling kindly at her.

"I'm just waiting for my aunt." Francesca wondered why she always felt like she had been caught
in the cookie jar at Belle Rose.

"Come along, I'll walk you back to the house."
He smiled down at her. "I was just at Lyre Hall.
I'm afraid it's time to start thinking about what's to
be done about young English's estate. Both houses
are masterpieces of architecture."

After those words Axel became preoccupied with
his thoughts and they walked back to the house in
silence with the pale winter sun casting weak shadows about them. Francesca suddenly felt a deep melancholy overtaking her as the cold wind from the
bay rushed against her, blowing her hair fiercely
back from her face. She looked upon all the beauty

that surrounded her, and her gaze fell long on Belle Rose as she strolled silently beside Axel Kingsly. Her eyes slowly glided out over the water where the *Sea Song* sat, with its hidden mystery, turning slowly on its anchor. Francesca thought that even with all that money could buy, the Englishes and the Lynches could never find true happiness.

"The *Sea Song* looks lonely, doesn't she?" Francesca averted her eyes from the sight of the boat.

"I've mentioned to Mrs. Moore that perhaps she and Mr. Moore should take over Belle Rose. After all, they were very close friends with the English family." Axel waited for a response from Francesca.

"I suppose that that would be a good idea," she answered after thinking about it for a few moments.

"We shall see," Axel said.

"And what about Lyre Hall?" Francesca asked.

"I'm not certain of that, as yet," Axel answered. In the distance Francesca saw old Cyrus staring at them from behind a hedge.

Chapter Eleven

Friday arrived and Francesca's hopes rose again. Perhaps today Bud would be waiting for her in front of Lacy's. Next Tuesday she would receive her diploma and there would be no more Tuesday or Friday classes. If this was the way their relationship was to go on, if she could ever bring herself to admit it, it might be just as well that there would be no more endless waiting, which only brought disappointment and the feeling of emptiness. But today, she still hoped that Bud would be there. She never expected to see him in the morning, so her hopes would last until the afternoon.

Francesca thought to herself just how much could anyone possible care for someone they hardly knew. The whole thing was completely and absolutely absurd.

She walked up Pike Street steeling herself against the inevitable disappointment. But as she approached Lacy's, the follies of the heart rose with a whimper. She whispered, ''But I do love him.''

The awning of Lacy's was flapping again in the wind, its burden of snow dusted off and swept away. It was left with its lonely song in the air. There was not a soul nearby.

Francesca's heart skipped a beat when she saw Tom Lacy walk out and stand under the awning, arms akimbo. She hoped against all hope that he was waiting to tell her some news of Bud. She smiled cheerfully, even though misgivings were riding high in the pit of her stomach.

Tom Lacy smiled as he spoke. ''Hello, Francesca.'' He paused for a moment, a little embarrassed. ''May I call you Francesca? Bud's spoken so often of you that I feel we're old friends.''

''Please do.'' She smiled with the expectation that she was after all about to hear something that was sure to please her.

''Call me Tom.''

''Thank you.'' She was still smiling hopefully.

''Bud called the house this morning and asked me to tell you to wait here for him.'' Tom Lacy looked at his watch. ''He should be here soon. Come on in and have that cup of coffee we spoke about.''

He stood aside and held the door for Francesca as she walked through. Tom found a table in the corner for her and called a waiter over.

''Miss Mayhew is my guest.'' He looked down at Francesca. ''Order anything you like.''

''Thank you.'' Francesca was fairly lightheaded at the mere thought of seeing Bud soon. She ordered a cup of coffee and a piece of pastry that she found hard to swallow with so much excitement bubbling in her throat. She played idly with her coffee spoon. Suddenly a pair of rough hands slipped over her eyes and she felt a kiss on the top of her head. She laughed.

"Guess who?"

"I have no idea."

"Ahh, how soon we forget." Bud laughed and sat down across the table from her. "How have you been?" he asked.

"Very well. Just a little anxious about you." She lowered her eyes.

"I see you have coffee. Would you like another cup?"

"Yes, please."

Bud called the waiter, who plodded over to them. "Another coffee, and I'll have a beer."

"What have you been up to?" he asked, waiting for the waiter to return.

"Oh, just going to my classes and helping my aunts to pack away some things at the house of a friend of theirs who died."

"Oh." Bud looked uncomfortable and said, "I'm sorry."

"I didn't really know him, but it's difficult for my aunts. I think it has been an emotional upset for my Aunt Daisy. She hasn't been feeling well lately."

Bud cocked his head as he peered at her with some concern.

"We've had Dr. Rainer in to look at her, but he can't find anything wrong with her, so he just has her resting."

"How long has she been sick?" he asked.

"About two weeks." She looked worried. "That's rather a long time, isn't it?"

Bud sat contemplating Francesca for a moment. "Look, darling, I'm going to take you to the bus." He reached into his jeans pocket for money to pay the bill.

Francesca felt anger well up in her, and she said curtly, "I'm the guest of Tom Lacy."

"Oh." He smiled. "Then I'll just pay for mine. You and Tom are becoming good friends."

"Yes. I see more of him than I do you." Francesca was angry with herself immediately after she had spoken the words. "Oh, Bud, I'm sorry. It's just that I dream of being with you and it's always . . ." Her voice trailed off. "I just don't quite know what to make of all this," she ended.

Bud lifted her chin in his hand. "Please, Francesca, let me hold your dreams just a little longer." He smiled. "I promise they're safe with me."

While Francesca said good-bye to Tom Lacy, Bud went to the telephone booth that he had pointed out to her the first time that they had sat and talked together. The call was quick and he returned ready to take Francesca to the bus station. He said to Tom, "Something's come up. I'll speak to you later on tonight." And he practically pushed Francesca through the door. At the foot of the bus steps Bud looked up at her. "Soon, we will do all the nice things that you want to do." He kissed her hard on the lips. He did not wait for the bus to depart as he usually did. When Francesca reached her seat, she caught a fleeting glimpse of Bud running through the station back to where he had parked the rented car.

Francesca telephoned Amelia from the bus station and asked, ''Are you ready to go home?''

''No. I have a client coming in a few minutes. Will you be all right?''

''Oh, yes. I'll walk home.'' She smiled at Amelia over the phone. ''Walking will be good for me. See you soon.'' They said good-bye and Francesca started to walk up the hill from town to Holly Street.

A cold gray mist was rolling in from the bay, crawling over everything in its path, leaving bare branches and bushes as wet as if it had rained. Francesca was suddenly plunged into a deep melancholy as the ghostly mist wrapped its clammy arms around her. She became frightened and she did not know why, but fear was walking with her up the hill to Holly Street and she was almost in a panic to reach the door of the old Victorian house and the safety of its walls.

She was about to burst through the iron gate when she saw Ophelia Defoe coming down the walk, the gray mist almost obliterating her. Francesca brought her fear under control with a gulp of air and called a greeting to Ophelia who at the same moment saw Francesca.

''Francesca, I'm so glad you made it home safely in this pea soup.''

''Hello, Ophelia. Will you be able to get home safely in this awful mess?''

''I think so. I was just visiting Daisy. I'm more

than a little concerned for her. Dr. Rainer is their old family physician and I think that 'old' sums it up. I wish that I could suggest Robert, but, well, if she doesn't improve soon, I'm going to break a rule,'' she said somberly.

"Yes, I think it has been too long," Francesca said. "I don't know what Aunt Lelia thinks, but if she's not better in a few days, I would say go ahead."

"All right, dear, I'll keep in touch."

"Be careful, Ophelia," Francesca gave warning to Ophelia as she was swallowed up by the gray mist.

"I will," Francesca heard Ophelia's voice moving away, then the engine of her car started up and eased into the distance.

Francesca stood for a moment reflecting on the dense fog, seeing only her thoughts. The fear that she had felt coming up the hill was beginning to subside a bit, but some of it still clung to her like the fog.

She hoped that Amelia would come in soon. She started to walk up the path again and before she reached the door her concern for Amelia at last ended as she heard Amelia's car turn into the driveway.

Francesca walked to the side of the house and waited for Amelia. She called to her as she stepped from the car. "I'm glad that you're in."

"It was too foggy. My clients called and canceled for today." Amelia joined Francesca and they went into the house together where the warmth of the house dispelled some of Francesca's uneasiness.

Lelia was met coming from the kitchen with some hot soup for Daisy. She wore a black velvet ribbon tied around her snowy hair and there were dark circles around her piercing eyes, which were losing their "know all" look and beginning to take on a look of confusion.

"I'll take the soup up to Aunt Daisy," Francesca offered.

"No, dear, I'm going upstairs anyway." She thought for a moment. "Ruth has dinner ready. You can come up and speak to Daisy while she sets the table." The two young women walked up the steps behind Lelia, whose usual brisk footsteps were slowed by something that neither Francesca nor Amelia understood.

Hello, Aunt Daisy," they both said, going to the side of the bed and taking their aunt's hands in theirs.

"Are you feeling better?" Francesca asked.

"A little. I'm going to have some of Sally's soup that she makes so well. Charlotte insists that it will cure anything." Daisy smiled at the two young women. "Go now and have your dinner. Come up again after you've finished." She lay back weakly on the embroidered pillow case and closed her eyes for a moment. Francesca backed away from the bed. Fear was seizing her again and she saw the same look on Amelia's face.

The joy of seeing Bud had long since vanished

and she could not believe that she had felt such joy only a few hours ago.

Amelia and Francesca dined quietly together. They sat across the table from each other, neither knowing how to put into words the terrible thoughts that were haunting them.

''Ophelia was here this afternoon and she said that if Aunt Daisy does not improve in the next few days, she is going to ask Dr. Defoe to come in.'' Francesca spoke softly, playing with the food on her plate.

''I think that that is a good idea,'' Amelia replied.

''What is wrong, Amelia? Only a little while ago we were happy, all of us having dinner together, and now it's just you and me.'' Francesca bit her lip. ''I know that they are old, but not now, Amelia, not now. I don't think I could stand it if anything happened to them.''

''I know.'' Amelia bowed her head. ''Nothing will happen to them. We must believe that and not even talk about it.''

''You're right. I won't allow anything like that to enter my head.'' Francesca flung her hair back from her face where it had fallen in her moment of submission to fear. ''But I must tell you, Amelia, that for no reason at all this afternoon I was seized by a feeling of panic that I have never known before in my life.'' Almost as an afterthought, Francesca said, ''I saw Bud today.''

Amelia raised her eyebrows and asked, ''How is the mysterious Mr. Bud?''

''Still mysterious.'' She shrugged her shoulders.

"He practically threw me on the bus this afternoon and went dashing off someplace at a gallop."

"Well, don't feel too badly. I had a date with Bill and he called and asked if we could make it another night." She sighed. "We haven't decided on which night."

After dinner they helped Ruth clear away the dishes and looked in on Daisy, but she was asleep.

"I think I'll go through the new listings that we have for a while and see if I can come up with something for Mr. and Mrs. Ames for tomorrow," Amelia said.

"I think I'll read some." Francesca went into her room, leaving her door open in case Daisy awakened and needed something.

The book that Francesca picked up to read did not hold her interest, so she laid it down and got up and paced the floor before deciding to go up to the attic and visit the toys. For some reason, they gave her solace. Perhaps, she thought, it was going back to a gentler time when things at least seemed easier. If not altogether true, it let one of this age think so.

Francesca turned the light on at the bottom of the stairs. The ugly glare of the uncovered lightbulb threw a garish yellow light over the room. Francesca did not have to go any closer to see that the toys had been moved. The merry-go-round sat out in the floor and the dolls were scattered about, leaning over on their faces bottoms up instead of resting on chairs. The wicker doll buggy was empty of its blue-eyed china face, and the pillow where she had lain was thrust against the merry-go-round.

It was a subtle shock. Things were not in total disarray, just moved about carelessly. Francesca stood with her back to the wall as if she expected someone or something to rush past her. After a moment of disbelief, Francesca realized whoever had been there had left long ago. Gathering her wits, she ran down the hall to Amelia's room, whose door was also left open. Francesca called to her in a desperate whisper.

"Amelia, come with me. I want you to see something." Amelia flung her legs off the chaise longue and put the real estate book aside.

"What is it, Francesca?" Her first thoughts were that something was wrong with Daisy. "Is it Aunt Daisy?"

"No, it's in the attic." She pulled Amelia along, gripping her arm tightly.

"What's in the attic?" Amelia asked, bewildered by Francesca's urgency.

When they reached the top of the steps, Amelia looked around and asked, "Why, who's moved things about?"

"I don't know, but Amelia, someone is looking for something in this house." She spread her hands out. "But what?"

"Should we call the police?" Amelia asked.

"The problem is, there is nothing really to report to them. I can hear them in private conversation." Francesca made her voice very deep. " 'Those four old maids up there on Holly Street are seeing a man in the attic.' "

Amelia smiled ruefully and said, "That ain't funny, Francesca."

"But you do see that there is nothing that we can really tell them," Francesca made her point.

"Nothing's been stolen. What on earth is it that anyone could possibly want in this old house? We don't have any money hidden away. I thought that that was common knowledge around here." She grinned at Francesca. "We are what's known as genteel poor."

"So it has to be something other than money."

"Then again it might have been Aunt Lelia or Aunt Daisy."

"Or Ruth, for that matter, but I doubt it very much, considering those voices that I heard and the day that I was not feeling well and I thought I heard someone in the house." Francesca began picking up the toys and putting them back in place. Amelia joined her. Francesca stopped still for a moment, her eyes squinting in the realization of a thought that had just occurred to her.

"When I arrived home this afternoon Ophelia Defoe was just leaving, and now I remember that the night I heard voices up here she was not in the sitting room when I came down."

Francesca stopped, waiting for Amelia's thoughts to concur with hers. Amelia was not catching up with her, and Francesca did not seem to be making much sense. Then Amelia had an idea that might put Francesca's doubts about Ophelia to rest.

"Ophelia lived here for a while. She could have found whatever it is long ago. And neither was Fergus in the sitting room when you came down. And heaven knows, they both have access to the house. If they wanted anything they would only have to ask.''

''Amelia, I don't think it's that simple.''

''What would Ophelia want? She is what's known as a newcomer to Edgecombe, and until she has been here close to three hundred years, she's not considered to be part of whatever intrigues might have gone on here. And no doubt there were quite a few.''

''Where did Ophelia come from?'' Francesca asked.

''New York. She wasn't born there, but she has a relative, a Mrs. Hyde, who is a friend of Aunt Daisy's. Aunt Daisy was visiting Mrs. Hyde when she met Ophelia there. Ophelia was tired of New York, so Aunt Daisy invited her here and she stayed for a while until she got a job with Dr. Defoe. After that she got a little apartment in town, and she and Dr. Defoe fell in love and got married.

''Well, it does seem that if she wanted anything she could have gotten it when she lived here.'' Another thought occurred to Francesca. ''Unless she left something here from her past that she doesn't want anyone to know about.''

''I don't know, Francesca,'' Amelia concluded.

They finished putting the toys back into their proper places and went down to Amelia's room, two very perplexed young women.

Francesca and Amelia agreed not to speak to Daisy and Lelia about what they thought was going on in the house. Francesca observed that Lelia was not looking well either and that she had slowed down considerably. Her brisk vitality seemed to have been ebbing day by day. Her straight shoulders were beginning to droop. The happy sound of the house had vanished and the hushed tones of sickness now pervaded.

Chapter Twelve

The last day of Francesca's classes arrived and she found herself accepting her certificate all alone. No one had been able to attend the little graduation, and Francesca felt lonely. She walked for the last time up Pike Street, passing Lacy's without a glimpse of Tom Lacy or Bud.

That evening Francesca and Amelia sat in the drawing room talking quietly over a cup of coffee.

"I think it's time we called Dr. Defoe in. Aunt Daisy is not getting better, she's getting worse, regardless of what Dr. Rainer says about resting," Francesca said as Amelia reached for the telephone on the table.

"Hello, Ophelia, this is Amelia." Francesca knew that Ophelia was making social amenities as she heard Amelia say, "Very well, thank you. Well, that's why I'm calling you. No, she's not improving, and Francesca and I feel it's time that she saw someone else." There was a pause. "Tonight?" Amelia held the phone to her chest and turned to Francesca.

"Ophelia wants Dr. Defoe to come over tonight."

"I think we have waited too long already. Tell her yes."

As soon as Amelia put the receiver back, the telephone rang again. Francesca answered as Amelia went to ready Daisy for Dr. Defoe.

"Hello." Surprise radiated on Francesca's face. "Bud?" She could not believe her ears. Bud was actually telephoning her as if it was nothing out of the ordinary. But the tone of his voice soon told her otherwise.

"Francesca, I can't talk, but how is your aunt?"

"Not very well, I'm afraid."

"Do me a favor and take your aunt to the hospital."

"We've just called Dr. Defoe and he will be here shortly."

"Get your Aunt ready and drive her to the hospital. Tell Defoe to meet you there."

Confusion rippled through Francesca's body and she thought she might be losing her mind.

"Promise me, Francesca, that you will take her to the hospital. I've got to go now." He paused for a moment. "I'll see you soon." He hung up and Francesca stood staring at the receiver. She put the phone back in the cradle and ran up the stairs.

"Amelia!" Amelia came out of Daisy's room in answer to Francesca's call. "I've just had the strangest call from Bud. He asked me how my aunt was and I told him not very well, and he made me promise to take her to the hospital right away and have Dr. Defoe meet us there. I don't know what Bud knows about this sickness, but I think we should take her to the hospital. Come on, I'll get her robe and slippers. We can put her coat over her nightgown.''

''You trust Bud this much?'' Amelia looked at Francesca questioningly.

''I think so, and if he's an alarmist, then there's no harm done. But if we delay taking her, then we might be in trouble.''

When they arrived at the hospital with Daisy and an unsteady Lelia, Dr. Defoe was waiting for them at the emergency entrance. He took one look at Lelia and said that he wanted both women admitted. They were wheeled to a room with two beds with a very nervous Francesca and Amelia following behind in a slow run. The rush down the hospital corridor brought back unbearable memories to Francesca of the day she had rushed down another hospital corridor with the chargé d'affaires, only to be told that it was too late. Her parents had both died instantly.

Daisy and Lelia were put to bed and the door closed on Francesca and Amelia, who sat huddled together on the windowsill. Tears ran down Francesca's cheeks and she bowed her head, her thick hair falling around her face, hiding the agony of the fear of that moment and past memories. Sobs shook her shoulders and Amelia, knowing how fresh the memories were, cradled Francesca in her arms. Francesca managed to speak through her sobs.

''I just want to cry for a minute.''

''Go ahead, Francesca, cry.''

After what seemed forever Dr. Defoe came out of the room pushing his stethoscope into the pocket of his white coat. He viewed Francesca and Amelia with gentle concern. "I'm not sure, but I think I know what it is. We will start making some tests in the morning. Now, I want you two young ladies to go home and try to get some rest. It's going to be a busy day for you tomorrow. I want both of you here in the morning at ten o'clock. I should have some preliminary reports by then." He paused for a moment with a thought. "In fact, I think that I will stay here for the rest of the night and see what I can come up with before the lab people get here."

Francesca and Amelia thanked Dr. Defoe and started back to Holly Street.

"Darn this fog," Amelia said, trying to peer through the thick vaporous haze.

Getting back home took twice the time that it would have ordinarily and both Francesca and Amelia breathed a sigh of relief when Amelia swung the small car into the driveway. As the headlights swept through the shrubbery, Francesca caught the dark figure of a man darting back from the beams of the headlights.

"Amelia!" Francesca gulped in a breath of air. "I just saw a man standing in the bushes."

"You did?" Frightened, Amelia asked, "It wasn't our neighbor Mr. Bailey, was it?"

"No, Mr. Bailey is heavyset, isn't he?"

"Yes." Amelia took the keys from the ignition hurriedly. "Lock your side. I have my keys, so all we have to do is make a dash for the door."

"Oh, no, I hope there's no one inside."

"Francesca, you do know how to instill confidence,'' Amelia said dryly. They made a unified dash for the front door, shutting it quickly behind them.

Breathlessly, Francesca said, ''It's funny, all of our fears are based on supposition. We can't call the police and say that we saw a man standing in the shadows. They would say that he was just waiting for the car to pass.'' Francesca bit into her bottom lip, almost drawing blood, and fell into a disturbing thought. ''Do you know, Amelia, the man standing in the shadows reminded me of Bud.''

''Bud!'' Amelia's mouth flew open and stayed that way for a moment. ''Why on earth would he lurk around here?'' She smiled. ''Unless he just wants to make sure his little Francesca is safe and sound.'' She shrugged her shoulders. ''But then why not just call?''

Francesca and Amelia went through the house and saw that nothing had been disturbed, set the alarm clock for 7:30, and went to bed for a restless night.

Dr. Defoe was waiting for Amelia and Francesca in his office. They both feared what he might tell them and when they saw the worried expression on his face, their hearts sank.

''What is it, Dr. Defoe?'' Francesca asked.

''There is something very curious here and I want you both to think hard. A lot will depend on your answers.''

Francesca could feel her Gaylord blood rise up, and in her mind her voice sounded like that of Lelia's, saying *''Get on with it, man.''* But when she spoke, she said, "Yes, of course. What is it that you wish to know?"

Dr. Defoe pressed his lips together until they were just a white line. He shuffled some papers around on his desk and finally said, "Can either of you think of any way your aunts could have ingested arsenic?"

Amelia and Francesca gasped at the same time. "Arsenic?"

"How could that be?" Francesca asked as a wave of shock spread over her face.

The first shock wave that hit Francesca began to subside and reason ebbed back. "Aunt Daisy does a lot of gardening. Does she use arsenic as an insecticide? Particularly for her roses?"

"I've never seen any," Amelia stated.

Dr. Defoe leaned forward on his desk. "They will be all right. Daisy had more in her system then Lelia, but I can tell you that time was running out. A little later and there might have been too much damage." He smiled. "But I'm happy to say that everything is now under control." He frowned. "We have to find the source." He got up from his desk. "Think hard, as hard as you can, search the place, and see what you can come up with."

The word "search" sent a shiver through Francesca and it suddenly occurred to her that this whole affair might be more dangerous then she had ever dreamed.

"Well, thank you so much for the good news, Dr. Defoe," Francesca heard herself saying. "And we will certainly start looking the moment we get home."

"Very good. Then I'll expect to hear from you soon. And remember, anything and everything, gardening materials, powders, sprays, read the ingredients on labels." He repeated, "Everything."

"Certainly," Amelia agreed, still in a state of bewilderment.

Amelia and Francesca stopped in to see Daisy and Lelia, leaving Ruth with the sisters. They took what they thought their aunts would need for the few days' stay in the hospital. They did not visit very long, feeling the urgency to find the source of the poison, but they did promise to return again at visiting hours that afternoon.

In the car Amelia came back to reality. "I'll drop you off at home and you can start looking. I'll have to go to the office for a while, then I'll be back to help with . . ." She was at a loss for words. ". . . whatever we have to do, Francesca." She quickly fought back the tears that were welling in her eyes.

Amelia let Francesca out at the curb. "I'll see you in a little while." The little car pulled away and vanished down the hill.

Francesca let herself in, and leaned with her back against the door. She tried to imagine the best place to start first. She almost wished that Ruth had come back with her, as the silence played a deafening symphony around her. She started up the stairs when from a sideways glance into the sitting room she saw some papers scattered on the sofa. She backed down one step and slowly opened the door wider.

Francesca did not deceive herself. She was afraid to be in the house alone. When she pushed the door open her heart gave one loud thump and she stopped in dismay. Papers were scattered over the tabletops and every drawer had been pulled out and left gaping open, their contents half in, half out. Fear rose in Francesca's throat and choked her. Her first thoughts were to flee the house as fast as she could, but regaining a minimum of courage, she called out, "Anyone here?" Later on she thought that had been fairly stupid.

Bracing herself, Francesca walked up the stairs. She peered into Daisy's room and was horrified at the disarray. Clothing had been pulled from closets and bureau drawers. A small black strongbox that an active two-year-old could have opened had been pried open, its contents strewn across Daisy's bed, mixed with her personal clothing. Francesca saw her beautiful blue silk slip thrown on the floor and her precious volumes of poetry pulled from their Persian box and scattered asunder.

Francesca clasped her hands to her mouth and ran down the stairs and out of the house to the Baileys' next door, where she telephoned the police and Amelia and asked her to come home.

Mr. Bailey waddled back to the house with Francesca. Noting Mr. Bailey's girth, Francesca thought the man caught in the beams of the headlights was certainly not Mr. Bailey. She would mention the slim man to the police.

Amelia dashed from the car just as Francesca and Mr. Bailey reached the front door. A frantic Amelia joined them on the porch, her hair flying about her face, which bore the strain of an unknown fear.

Amelia walked around the house exclaiming as she looked at each violation of her home.

"Oh, no. Oh, no." Francesca put her arms around Amelia and tried to comfort her, as well as herself.

After going through the house, the policemen gathered in the kitchen with notebooks opened and pens poised to write down anything that might help them. This was an unusual investigation for the Edgecombe Police Department, who mostly gave out traffic citations or occasionally picked up a library book from a delinquent borrower when Miss Pimm became concerned about one of her books.

The two officers were part of a five-man force, two each on duty day and night and the fifth always the backup if one was sick or on vacation. The two men sat down at the kitchen table. The officer with the round stomach and ruddy face, who seemed to be in charge, asked Francesca and Amelia if anything that they could see was missing.

"Nothing," Amelia answered.

"Nothing that I can see," Francesca echoed Amelia.

"Francesca did see a strange man standing near the driveway last night when we arrived back from the hospital."

"Oh?" The chief officer, whose name was Congers, turned to Francesca with a question in his voice.

"I didn't get a good look at him. He just seemed tall and rather slim. He moved away quickly when the headlights caught him."

Congers ran his hands through his thinning sandy hair and said, ''This beats the heck out of me.''

''Me, too,'' the other officer agreed. ''What were you doing at the hospital?''

''We took Aunt Lelia and Aunt Daisy.'' Francesca sat down, her legs becoming too weak to support her. ''Chief Congers,'' she said weakly, ''our aunts have arsenic poisoning. Dr. Defoe thinks that it might be from some of Aunt Daisy's gardening materials. Amelia and I are supposed to look around and see if we can find anything containing arsenic.''

''Oh, no,'' Congers said. ''Luke, look out in the shed and see if there's any arsenic powder or in any compounds.''

''Okay, Chief.'' Luke went out the back door.

''How are Miss Lelia and Miss Daisy?''

''They're doing very well. Dr. Defoe said that we got Aunt Daisy there just in time,'' Amelia said.

The back door shoved open. They thought that it was Luke returning, but it was Mrs. Bailey with a pot of coffee.

''Thank you, Mrs. Bailey. Is it all right if I get some cups?'' Francesca asked the chief.

''Yeah, go ahead,'' he answered absently, playing with a pencil against his teeth.

Amelia and Francesca poured coffee for the policemen and Mr. and Mrs. Bailey. They were relieved that Mr. Bailey was staying with them.

''Francesca, you and Amelia come over to the house for dinner and I will make up the guest room for you tonight,'' Mrs. Bailey said, going out the back door again.

Luke came through the door, holding it for Mrs. Bailey.

"I don't see nothing out there, Chief, mostly plain fertilizer. Ain't much of nothing in the shed." Luke held up some little plastic bags. "I took some samples in case you want to send some of it over to the lab in Eton."

"Okay. Have a cup of coffee." Congers began wrapping things up. "You two young ladies stay at the Baileys' tonight, just so you'll feel better."

"Chief," Francesca spoke nervously, "we have to go back to the hospital soon and we would rather not tell Aunt Lelia and Aunt Daisy about this. It might upset them too much."

"I don't see any reason to say anything to them for the time being. I just want to speak to Dr. Defoe for a minute or two."

"What about Ruth?" Amelia asked, looking at Francesca.

"Perhaps we can take some things to her and ask Dr. Defoe to let her stay at the hospital tonight under the pretense that it's for the comfort of Aunt Daisy and Aunt Lelia," Francesca offered.

"Good idea, and I would like to take Mrs. Bailey up on her offer," Amelia agreed.

"Me, too." Francesca gave a sigh of relief.

"Can we start to clean up now, Sheriff?" Amelia asked.

"Sure, go ahead. I tried dusting for fingerprints. I have a few, but I'll bet they all belong to you folks." The chief gathered up his belongings, clearly bewildered by the whole business. This was what he read about in the newspapers and he never expected to be bothered with any of those big-city doings. That was why he liked Edgecombe—no excitement. Closing the door behind him, he thought, *If this keeps up, a person could get shot.* This was not his idea of police work. Riding around all day giving out a traffic ticket or two, picking up a library book for crazy Miss Pimm—why, he didn't even arrest drunks, he just took them home.

Congers slammed the patrol car's door behind him irritably, gave a heavy sigh, and said to Luke, shaking his head at his misfortune, ''Let's head over to the doctor's office.''

Chapter Thirteen

Though small, Edgecombe was not too small to abound with distorted news of what had occurred on Holly Street. The rumor that went around town was that the house had been broken into, and the burglar had so upset the Gaylord sisters that they had to be hospitalized.

Francesca and Amelia felt that this was as good a tale as any and actually made more sense than whatever the true story was, so they never made any clear-cut comments on the actual event that took place.

The test from the laboratory in Eton showed no trace of anything that should not have been in Daisy's gardening supplies. As a suggestion the chief asked them to tell as few people as possible about the arsenic.

"I don't think anyone is trying to do away with your aunts, mind you. It's probably from some harmless source. But until we find out where it's coming from, the less said the better."

142

The chief sucked some wind through his teeth, still finding it hard to believe that he was playing the role of a real cop. He went back to his office and kicked the wastebasket clear across the room.

''They know what to do in the movies. I don't.'' He crammed his hat down on his head and went down to Cary's tavern, sat down in a back booth, and ordered a beer.

Charlotte visited the hospital every day. For five days the long black limousine stood parked in a restricted area until she returned.

''This is awful, simply awful. What is this world coming to? We're going to have to start bolting our doors the way they do in New York.'' She fussed about Lelia and Daisy like a mother hen. ''I asked Francesca and Amelia to come and stay with me until they felt better, but they were quite brave and insisted that they weren't afraid to stay in the house. I must say, I would have been. Well, you're going home today. Jeffers is waiting downstairs for us.'' She mused, ''I'm sure it was just a random burglary and it's perfectly safe now.''

Dr. Defoe came into the room, followed by Francesca and Amelia. His trained eyes swept over his two patients professionally and then as an old friend.

''You both look fine,'' he said. ''Unfortunately, we still don't know the source of the arsenic. Be careful of what you eat and keep a record for a while.'' He smiled. ''We don't want to slip up. See me in my office in a few days. Good day, ladies.''

Dr. Defoe had left them with a nagging thought as he left on his rounds. He returned a moment later.

"You know, your improvement was so rapid because you were totally free of poison in the hospital. It's in your home." His hand still resting on the doorknob, he smiled. "I wasn't sure that I had stressed that enough. Thought I'd better reiterate this in no uncertain terms. We don't want you back here. . . . See you in a few days." He closed the door and left them with even more chilling thoughts.

Settled back home, Lelia gave Francesca and Amelia a curious stare.

"You didn't tell us that the house had been burglarized."

"Oh! Who told you?" Francesca was annoyed.

"Charlotte, of course," Lelia replied.

"We simply didn't want to worry you. You had enough to contend with, and nothing was taken. Chief Congers went over everything with us and there was nothing missing."

"Humph! Ellis Congers knows less about being chief than I do." Lelia grunted, but Francesca noticed a sly glance between Lelia and Daisy that had some sort of special meaning.

They sat around the dinner table, things almost back to what Francesca had called "happier days." Lelia patted her mouth with her napkin.

"Would you two mind very much if Daisy and I took a little holiday? Just for a few days." She glanced again at Daisy. "I think we need to get away for a little while."

"Why, that's a splendid idea, don't you think so, Amelia?"

"Yes, and when you get back we might have found the source of the arsenic. Yes, I think that's a very good idea. I'm sure Dr. Defoe will be pleased." Amelia was as pleased as Francesca, because Dr. Defoe had said that the source was in the house.

"And when you come back, everything will be all right," Francesca said.

"Then it's settled. We'll leave next Monday. I think we should be strong enough by then."

"Where will you go?" Francesca asked.

"There's a lovely inn in Vermont that we used to go to. What do you think of that, Daisy?"

"Lovely, Lelia." Daisy smiled, pleased.

On Sunday night Francesca and Amelia, with the aid of Ruth, helped Lelia and Daisy to pack. Dr. Defoe had found their conditions much improved and was indeed pleased with their rapid recovery. But he would not have advised a trip just yet and that was precisely why they had not mentioned it to him.

Lelia and Daisy boarded a small commuter plane in Eton for Boston where they were to change to an Air New England flight that would take them to Bennington, Vermont. They bade Amelia and Francesca good-bye, saying that they would call when they arrived at the inn. But in Boston they transferred to a plane that landed them at New York's LaGuardia Airport. They walked to the Allegheny ticket window and bought two tickets to Philadelphia.

In Philadelphia, Lelia and Daisy took a taxi directly to the law firm of Hadley, Wilkes and Morrow. They marched with shoulders erect through the heavy mahogany doors with a highly polished brass plate bearing the name of the partners. A receptionist who blended harmoniously with the staid and elegant room greeted them with a solicitous smile. Lelia walked briskly up to the ornately carved desk.

"Misses Daisy and Lelia Gaylord to see Mr. Hadley, please."

The sisters were admitted to Mr. Hadley's office without delay and Mr. Hadley greeted them with outstretched hands.

"Lelia! Daisy! It's so good to see you." He grinned broadly. "It's nearing that time." He sighed, fingering the pockets in his vest.

"Yes, Andrew. Amelia will be twenty-five in another month. So I believe that we should get all of our papers together. Daisy and I are not getting any younger." Mischief gleamed in Lelia's eyes and she said humorously, "And neither are you."

"Well, everything is in order." He smiled.

That evening Daisy and Lelia checked into a small but good hotel, removed their hats, and drew in a deep breath. Daisy reached for the telephone beside the bed and dialed the operator and gave her the telephone number on Holly Street.

Francesca's voice came over the wire. "Hello, Aunt Daisy. How was your flight?"

"Lovely flight, dear. Everything is quite nice. Your Aunt Lelia and I will have some supper and rest for a while. Are you and Amelia all right?"

"Oh, yes, don't worry about us. Bill Adams

stopped by for a while. So we're just fine; we just want you to rest and get better.'' Francesca paused for a moment to look for a pen to write with. ''We don't have your telephone number.'' She had the pen set to write down the number when Daisy suddenly said, ''Oh, dear, Lelia's calling me to supper. I don't have my glasses nearby, but we will call you tomorrow. Give my love to Amelia. Good night, dear.

Francesca was left holding the receiver in one hand and a pen in the other and a steady buzzing in her ear.

Daisy looked at Lelia. ''At least I didn't have to lie. Well, not very much,'' she added.

''Soon it will all come to a close.'' Lelia smiled at her sister.

''Yes. Where did the years go?''

A light suddenly flashed in Lelia's eyes and she picked up the telephone.

''I don't see why we should stay in Philadelphia for six more days.'' She tapped the table with her index finger, while waiting for the operator to answer. When the voice answered, ''May I help you?'' Lelia replied, ''Will you get the airport for me, please?'' She smiled. ''Why not go to that little inn in Vermont?''

A week to the day that Lelia and Daisy left Edgecombe they arrived back, rested and in the best of health. Francesca and Amelia met them at the airport and were very pleased with the rejuvenated appearance of their aunts.

"No more burglary attempts, I hope," Lelia greeted them fondly with a bit of a tease in her voice.

Amelia and Francesca looked sheepish.

"You weren't supposed to know about that." Francesca grinned. Lelia laughed. "Keep a secret in Edgecombe? Don't be naive, Francesca." She gave a snort. "And what Ellis Congers knows about being a policeman you could put on the head of a pin."

Just as they pulled into the driveway, Charlotte's limousine pulled up to the curb. Characteristically flawless, in a smoke gray mink coat, she alighted from the car with the aid of her driver.

"Oh, Daisy and Lelia. I couldn't wait to see you." Scrutinizing her old friends carefully, she said, "You look marvelous—rest was exactly what you needed."

The house seemed to be getting back to normal. There had been no more mysterious intrusions and Francesca was getting ready to take Florence's place at the Benson Realty office. She had not heard another word from Bud since his strange phone call when he had been so crucially accurate. Amelia and Bill were getting along splendidly and there was certainly a blossoming romance in the now-calm air as Amelia settled into a stable relationship with Bill. It was becoming a natural habit and she glowed with the joy of new love. While Francesca pined quietly for Bud, she went about the the ordinary business of day-to-day living.

Francesca bought a used car in Eton. When she first went to shop for one, she stopped in the tavern to say hello to Tom Lacy, hoping that he might have some word of Bud, but that had been fruitless. She boarded the bus back to Edgecombe with the fear that she might never see Bud again.

There was another nagging fear gripping Francesca. After the return of Daisy and Lelia from Vermont, they seemed back to perfect health again, but for the last week she thought she noticed a change. They were slowing down again. She wanted to ask Amelia if she had noticed it, but Amelia was so busy with Bill that she hardly ever saw her. Francesca did not want to sound as if she was becoming paranoid, but she felt her senses becoming keenly alert and she remembered her father telling her, ''Follow your gut feelings, honey. They're there for a reason.'' But she did not know from which direction the warning bell was sounding.

When she arrived home Charlotte and Ophelia were paying a call. They were sitting in the drawing room having tea where Francesca joined them. Her eyes fell immediately on Daisy, who looked wan and had the beginnings of dark smudges under her eyes again. Lelia was only a little less than her usual self.

''Hello, Charlotte, Ophelia,'' she spoke absently as she went to Daisy and gave her a slight hug as her eyes examined her secretly.

''How are you, Francesca?'' Charlotte asked. ''I suppose you're nearly ready to start working with Amelia,'' she said unconvincingly. ''That should be nice.'' She smiled over the rim of her cup.

''I think so, too, Francesca,'' Ophelia spoke with sincerity. ''I think I might try my hand at real estate.

I believe women make the best salespeople for houses.'' She drew her shoulders up. ''I think we love houses more, don't you?''

''I think so.'' Francesca laughed, agreeing with Ophelia's theory. ''When I looked with Mother and Dad we were always more successful with a saleswoman.'' She laughed again. ''Let's hope that this theory proves true.''

''I'm sure you will do well, Francesca.'' Charlotte smiled. ''I'm just not quite certain that I approve of young ladies working.''

Francesca smiled back at Charlotte. ''Most of the time it's necessary.''

''Well do I know that,'' Ophelia chimed in with a wave of her hand in the air.

''Humm-mm,'' was Charlotte's only reply. ''Well, I must leave.'' She rose, gathering up her purse. ''Remember,'' she spoke to Lelia and Daisy, ''to take some of Sally's broth. It will do you a world of good. I'll pick the crock up another time. No need to bother emptying it now.''

Daisy rose from her chair a little unsteadily. ''Thank Sally for us, won't you?'' She started to the door with Charlotte, and Lelia followed. Francesca went ahead to retrieve Charlotte's coat from the hall closet. She felt the softness of the fur.

''What a lovely coat,'' Francesca said to Charlotte as she helped her on with her coat.

''Bear in mind,'' Charlotte said as she pointed her finger playfully at Francesca, ''you will not get one working at Benson's.''

''I'll keep that in mind.'' Francesca laughed.

Ophelia had remained seated in the sitting room watching the flames dance in the grate. When the three women returned and took their seats again Ophelia asked, ''Have you been to see Robert lately?''

''Why, not since we returned from Vermont,'' Daisy answered. Ophelia stood up in preparation to leave. ''Why don't you make an appointment for a follow-up?''

''I think that that's a good idea,'' Francesca spoke up. ''I'll make the appointment in the morning.''

Dr. Defoe did not like what he saw. A puzzled frown creased between his pale eyes.

''Daisy, Lelia, I'm going to put both of you back into the hospital for a few days. We are going to have to find out where you're picking up this poison.'' Dr. Defoe was thoughtful. ''It's odd that Francesca and Amelia aren't affected.'' He reached for the telephone. ''I'm going to have someone go out to the house and get some paint samples sent to the lab for test. Do you remember the American ambassador in Italy who was being poisoned by chips of paint falling from her bedroom ceiling? The paint contained arsenic. That might be the answer.''

Dr. Defoe looked pleased with his new theory. ''That might just be it.'' But the thought still lingered in his mind. ''But why not Francesca and Amelia?''

Again Francesca was sinking into dark caverns. Her hope of hearing from Bud crushed, and the only security in her life, her aunts, was being threatened. In this moment of despair Francesca took a stand

and she vowed that she would find out what this was that was eating away at her foundation. Enough had been taken away from her, and everyone had a right to some peace in this world.

Once again Francesca found herself packing little things to take to Daisy and Lelia who were already showing remarkable improvement after only two days in the hospital. Ruth helped her with small toiletries and found books for them to read.

Ruth opened the refrigerator. ''We may as well take the fruit.'' She looked at the crock that contained Sally's famous broth. ''What about this soup Mrs. Moore brought?'' Francesca thought for a moment. ''It's been there for a while. Let's throw it out.''

''Mrs. Moore thinks that it can cure anything that ails you.'' Ruth chuckled.

''I know,'' Francesca agreed. ''But it's a bit old. We don't need to add ptomaine poisoning to the arsenic.''

Ruth shuffled over to the sink and poured the broth out. ''If you ask me, I think it's a lot of hogwash,'' she said, washing out the crock.

Francesca smiled. She thought Ruth was a little jealous of all the fuss made over Sally's soup.

Chapter Fourteen

Francesca left Daisy and Lelia a bit disgruntled at having to be in the hospital again, but otherwise in good spirits. Ruth had returned home and she was left alone.

Loneliness had Francesca in its vise as she walked along the streets of Edgecombe. Feeling desperately sorry for herself, she headed toward the bay. She walked along the sodden sand leaving deep footprints trailing behind her, the wind fanned the hat that she wore low over her brow and the icy air brought the blood to her cheeks and the tip of her nose. Francesca felt the fire of restless desire for the beauty of love, its tenderness and warmth and the glowing sensation that set memories into motion for a lifetime. Her eyes traveled out over the bay where the *Sea Song* danced its endless dance on the waves that were stirred by the wind, its white hull melting into the gray mist. Even the cry of the gulls that soared overhead weaving in and out of surging dark clouds was muted in the heavy air and rang with irritation in their tedious and endless search for food.

Francesca was nearing Lyre Hall and Belle Rose. She hoped that she would not see old Cyrus. She hated being the object of his hooded, supicious eyes, which secretly searched for some hidden reason for her being on English property.

Braced against the wind, Francesca forged ahead to no place in particular. The lusty winds rushed against her face. Through the mist Francesca saw the tall figure of a man standing near the water's edge. As she drew near to him, he turned and faced her and her heart nearly exploded in her chest. Squinting her eyes, she tried to discern the almost-obscured figure.

It can't be Bud, she reasoned, trying to slow the rate of her heartbeat down to normal. The man was now walking at an easy pace toward her. Now she could see him clearly, and it was Bud. She started to run, struggling with the dense wet sand that tried to drag her feet under its soggy grains.

As Francesca advanced toward Bud, her pride became primary and took command over her heart as she felt anger rising above the joy of seeing Bud again. She wondered about this man as she approached him. He appeared in her life at odd moments and then disappeared again just as quickly.

Her footsteps slowed down and she glided up to him. He bent to kiss her on the lips, but she averted her head and his kiss fell upon her brow. Bud coughed playfully, knowing that Francesca was angry with him.

"How have you been?" he asked softly.

"I have been well. Thank you." She drew in a breath, starting to walk again. Bud fell in step with her. Francesca pushed her hands deep into the pockets of her coat.

"My aunts are back in the hospital, though."

"Oh?" A worried frown creased Bud's forehead.

"They're improving and should be home soon." She gazed up at Bud.

"How did you know that they were dangerously ill?" she asked. The question was filled with suspicion as their eyes locked.

He coolly replied, "For the moment chalk it up to male intuition."

"I hardly find that's an answer," Francesca said, equally as cool, and she found that they were having their first tiff.

"How far are you planning to walk?" he asked, as if his patience was beginning to wear thin and he was anxious to be on his way.

Francesca looked up at Belle Rose and as she passed she saw Cyrus dressed in a black slicker againt the wet mist watching as always, his hooded eyes hidden under the fisherman's rain hat. He looked like a dark sentinel on guard. Bud glanced up at the old man without a word.

"I can walk by myself," Francesca said, her cheeks growing warm.

"All right," Bud said and fell behind her. When Francesca turned to see where he was, he was nowhere to be seen. She stood for a moment wrapped in confusion. Tears stung her eyes and she thought,

I don't care if I never see him again. And the next time Charlie Baxter called and asked her to dinner, she would certainly accept his invitation. She wiped a hot tear away quickly and resolutely she turned around and started back to town. The thought occurred to Francesca that perhaps Bud did not really exist, that somehow he was a figment of her imagination. Francesca heaved a deep sigh of relief. Tom Lacy knew him, but he was the only one and no one else knew Tom Lacy except her.

Lelia and Daisy were released from the hospital in the late morning, none the worst for wear, but Dr. Defoe had given even stricter orders that everything that they ate was to be recorded no matter what, or how little, so that if the poison showed up again they would know specifically what to examine.

Charlotte brought them home. It was agreed that her car was more comfortable than Amelia's small one.

They all went to the sitting room and Ruth brought tea.

Amelia arrived home early wearing the bloom of love and the sense of well-being. Her aunts were on the road to recovery and life seemed good again to the family on Holly Street.

When Francesca had a moment alone with Amelia in the kitchen, she asked teasingly, ''And how are things with Bill?''

Amelia raised her eyes to the ceiling. ''Oh! it couldn't be better.'' She smiled brightly.

Francesca peered down at her hands. "I saw Bud the other day."

"Oh! How wonderful, Francesca." Amelia was delighted at the news.

"No! I've decided that there cannot be anything between Bud and me." She looked at Amelia with eyes that filled with tears. "You know, Amelia, if you truly cared for someone you would want to share every little thing with that person." She turned away from Amelia and gazed through the kitchen window. "Bud obviously does not feel that way about me."

Amelia put her arm around Francesca. Turning her around to face her, she held her at arm's length. "This Bud is a fool. Why, you are one of the most beautiful women I have ever seen. In every way you are kind, and caring, and believe me, and when you've met someone else, he will be very sorry that he let you slip through his fingers." She tried to look into Francesca's bowed face. Seeing the tears glisten in the lovely walnut-brown eyes, Amelia said, almost in an oath, "The man is stupid." She went to the counter and unplugged the electric percolator. At that moment Charlotte entered the kitchen.

"I'll take the crock now." She felt the tenseness as she came through the door and her yes went from Amelia to Francesca.

"Is there anything wrong, Francesca, Amelia?"

"Oh, no, Charlotte, it's just been a bit of a strain." Francesca blinked away the tears. "I'm all right now."

"I understand, my dear," Charlotte said.

"Oh, I gave Jeffers the crock a few days ago," Francesca said.

"Very good; I didn't know. I must leave now."

"You have been very kind, Charlotte. Thank you so much."

There was a flicker in Charlotte's eyes and she said, "Daisy and Lelia and I go far back." She patted Francesca on the hand and started to go down the steps. But just then the mailman opened the iron gate with a clang and came up the brick path.

"Good morning, Mrs. Moore. Good morning, Miss Mayhew." he said, handing the mail to Francesca. "Another gray day," he commented, looking up at the sky.

"Good morning, Henry," Charlotte spoke, glancing at the mail in Francesca's hand. Francesca read the envelopes, frowning at one as she examined it closer. "This letter's from a law firm in Philadelpia. Hadley, Wilkes and Morrow. Oh, I do hope that Aunt Lelia and Aunt Daisy weren't so concerned about their health that they consulted a lawyer."

"Well, I must be going. Good-bye, dear." Charlotte walked briskly down the path to her car where Jeffers held the door open for her. Francesca watched as she disappeared in the back seat behind the dark glass.

When Francesca reentered the hall Amelia was helping Daisy and Lelia up the stairs. She dropped the mail on the hall table and went to assist with her aunts.

"I think they should take it a little at a time, don't you, Francesca?"

"Yes, and tomorrow you can come downstairs again and each day stay a little longer until you have all of your strength back," Francesca agreed.

"Really, Francesca, you and Amelia behave like two old hens," Lelia scolded them.

"Well, for the time being that's what we are," Francesca chided her.

After settling Lelia and Daisy into bed, Amelia and Francesca went back to the sitting room. Amelia asked, "Will you be all right alone? I have a client at two o'clock."

"Yes, of course," Francesca replied.

"I'm so glad that you haven't started work yet, and are still free to stay home with Ruth, whom I'm sure couldn't handle it alone."

"Poor Ruth," Francesca said. "It is hard on her."

"Let's help her with lunch and then I will have to go back to work." Amelia got up from the sofa, going to the kitchen where Ruth was preparing a salad for a light lunch.

Lunch was finished and Amelia went back to the office to meet her client. Francesca helped Ruth clear away the dishes, and a soundless lull had fallen over the house that hailed a depressing emptiness in Francesca. She looked in on Daisy and Lelia, who were sleeping soundly, and she suspected that Ruth too was napping in her room. She remembered that she had left the mail on the table downstairs and thought to get it so that when her aunts awakened she would have it upstairs. Francesca dropped the letters into the oversized pockets in the coat sweater that she wore.

She ran her hands through her thick hair. Unrest was building in her to the point of a scream and the afternoon stretched before her like a long road strewn with shadowy traces of gloom, and she thought, *Why is love laced with so much pain?*

Francesca did not feel like reading or watching anything on afternoon television. Francesca knew the only thing that would make this endless time pass a little quicker were the toys in the attic. She loved to search through them. Each time that she did, she invariably found something else exquisite. The last time she had found a quaint little music box that had carved figures on a merry-go-round. It excited her imagination as to what she might find this time.

Francesca gazed around the attic room, the silence of the room singing in her ears as a cold air stream stirred the old lace curtains at the small window. She left the attic door opened a crack so that she might hear Daisy or Lelia if they called, or the doorbell ring, and also to keep as much of the cold air as possible from escaping into the main part of the house without closing the door completely.

Francesca always had the feeling of going on an archaeological dig. Today, she thought she would dig deep behind the toys piled in the corner nearest the wall. She stepped gingerly into the midst of rag dolls and wooden carts, placing her feet wherever there was an empty space. She pushed the limp figures around until she had room to sit down, then she started meticulously to remove objects from their dusty hiding places of so many years. She was brushing away some of the dust from her fingers when she spotted a long dark cylinder hidden by years of dust and many little objects covered by what seemed the dust of time.

Francesca caught the end of the tube and carefully pulled it from under the things that were piled on top of it. She pulled the cap out and reached her fingers inside and felt a stiff fabric. She peered down the tube and tugged delicately at the article. It suddenly dawned on Francesca that it must be a painting and she became even more careful in removing it.

Standing up, Francesca spread the canvas over the toys. She could not believe her eyes as she ran her fingers over the surface of the painting, which after so long was virtually dust-free. She could feel the rise of the paint and she saw the mellow browns and the soft rendering of yellows. She stared into the transparent brown eyes that gazed serenely back into her own.

Francesca sat down abruptly and clasped her hands tightly together. ''Amazing—this looks like a Rembrandt.'' She looked down at the dark corner of the painting and saw very distinctly the signature REMBRANDT.

''How could this possibly be?'' she wondered. ''My aunts live in genteel poverty, and they have a Rembrandt painting stowed away in the attic.'' Francesca was too stunned to move. She heard a noise and turned quickly. She saw Charlotte standing over her with something in her hand. In the dim light it was impossible for Francesca to see what it was.

"Oh, Charlotte, you frightened me." She smiled and let out choked-up air with a sigh of relief. She peered closer at the old friend of her aunts and saw a look on her face which she did not understand, and for some reason, Francesca felt fear rise in her again.

"Did Ruth let you in?" she asked with a wary smile.

"No, she didn't." Charlotte spoke without her usual warmth.

"Oh." Francesca stood up. "Did I leave the door unlocked?"

"You have a letter that came today from Hadley's in Philadelphia. I'd like that letter." She stared coolly at Francesca.

"But why, Charlotte? Shouldn't my aunts see it first? The letter is addressed to them." Francesca stared back at Charlotte, not wanting to believe that she would actually make such a demand.

"You must have it with you." She held out her hand. "I've looked downstairs." Charlotte's head turned toward the door. "She's up here," she said with ice coating her words as Axel's head appeared over the railing. He moved up the steps until Francesca saw his full, elegantly clad body. He looked stern, but uncomfortable, but there was a determined air about him. He looked deadly serious about his mission. When he joined Charlotte he glared at her and said, "This is unfortunate."

"What could I do? She heard me come up behind her." Charlotte spoke defensively and self-righteously.

"See here, Francesca." Alex was going to try reasoning with her, as his voice became syrupy and conciliatory. ''There are some papers from Hadley's that are too important for two old ladies to understand, much less try to handle. It would be best for all to let me handle this matter. After all, I am a lawyer and you wouldn't want anyone to take advantage of your aunts with false information that would also harm English Shipping, now would you?''

''What business would Aunt Lelia and Aunt Daisy have with English Shipping?'' Francesca asked, disbelief spreading across her face at the threatening scene that was unfolding before her. ''I'm not at liberty to give you mail that is addressed to my aunts,'' she spoke with defiance.

Axel walked toward her with an outstretched hand. ''Then I'm afraid that I will have to insist. You see, with the death of Keal English, it is up to me and Fergus to look after the interests of English Shipping.''

''I repeat, Axel, what business would my aunts have with English Shipping, besides that of old family friends?'' Francesca felt anger flushing her cheeks, as the menacing character of Charlotte and Axel was also bringing fear to her.

Axel made a sudden lunge at Francesca, who quickly stepped aside, and Axel had difficulty righting himself again.

All eyes turned to the attic door as the voice of Daisy said loudly, ''What in the world is going on here?'' She was closely followed by Lelia, who swept up the tail of her black velvet dressing gown and mounted the steps with indignation, mingled with disbelief that such a scene was taking place under her roof. Anger racked her body as she strode toward Axel. She thought that her eyes were deceiving her when she saw him move threateningly at Francesca.

"Charlotte! Axel! What is the meaning of this?" she demanded.

Some sense of shame seemed to have invaded Charlotte's cold exterior as she backed away from the accusing stare of Lelia.

"Lelia, I must have the letter from Hadley's." She stumbled over the words.

"What letter?" Lelia asked, puzzled by Charlotte's demand.

"Aunt Lelia, a letter came this morning from a law firm, Hadley . . ." Francesca took the envelope from her pocket. ". . . Wilkes and Morrow," she said, handing the letter to Lelia.

"So, it's come." Lelia looked at the envelope with satisfaction.

"Yes, it has, and I will not let years of work go down the drain for anyone," Charlotte said, with venom seeming to trickle from her mouth.

"Take the letter, Axel."

"I wouldn't touch her, Axel, if I were you," a man's voice said, approaching the group of people who had suddenly become strangers. He came from the head of the stairs, and everyone had been too busy to notice. Words rang out simultaneously from Charlotte, Lelia, Daisy, and Francesca.

"Keal!"

"Bud!"

The three elderly women nearly collasped and Francesca was rendered speechless as she held on to her aunts, as much for support to herself as well as for them. Axel had gone ashen and Charlotte was as white as a sheet. For a moment they all hung suspended in an unbelievable moment; no one moved until Ophelia came up the steps and the scene that was frozen in time became fluid again and they moved in a dreamlike state before reality made its inevitable way back.

Daisy went to Keal with her heavy arms outstretched, tears streaming down her cheeks.

"Oh, Keal, darling, we thought you were dead." She embraced him and then cradled his face in her hands for a better appraisal of his features.

Keal put his arms around Daisy and said, as he looked over her head at Francesca, "I know, and I am sorry to have put you through this, but I had to find out who was trying to kill me."

Axel took advantage of the moment of reunion and tried to make a dash for the stairs, but Ophelia drew the smallest pistol that Francesca could have ever imagined existed, since she was not accustomed to seeing any sort of firearms. It fitted solidly in the palm of her gloved hand. She said calmly, "Don't try it, Axel. I will shoot you, you know." Her dry, matter-of-fact tone of voice made Axel think better of trying to make a break for it.

"Ophelia, you were never a lady," Charlotte said with disdain.

"Thank heaven for small things. Had I been a

lady I might have been exactly like you.'' Ophelia smirked.

Keal went to Francesca and tilted her chin up. He smiled down at her bewildered face and said, ''How do you do, Miss Mayhew, I'm Keal English. I hope that you will like me as much as you liked Bud.''

''You know Francesca?'' Lelia was as bewildered as Francesca.

''I've know her for a few months. I first met her in a storm coming up the hill from town. I was meeting Bill Adams. She nearly put my eye out with her umbrella.''

''That was you!'' Francesca said in astonishment.

Keal turned and grinned at Daisy and Lelia. ''She thought that I was shy about meeting you because I worked as a longshoreman, but I knew if I had walked her to the door you would have known it was me.''

''Didn't any of the workers recognize you?'' Francesca asked.

''No, they don't know anyone from the office,'' he answered.

''This has been a most unusual day,'' Daisy said, displacing a china doll from her chair and sitting down.

''The sheriff will be here soon,'' Keal said, looking at his watch.

A clattering of footsteps was heard in the hall moving toward the attic door. Fergus's round head appeared first, coming fast up the steps, then Chief Congers's face came next, wearing the most astounded expression.

Fergus saw Keal and his knees went weak.

"Keal, my boy. Where have you been?" He walked over to Keal and shook his hand.

The chief blinked in disbelief. "*English?*" he squawked. "We've been looking all over for you."

"Hello, Fergus." Keal took his hand warmly. He looked at Fergus with pity. "I'm afraid that I have bad news for you." Keal turned to the Chief, who stood like a statue, only his small blue eyes moving as they darted from person to person, his mouth gaping open.

"This is for you, Chief." Keal walked to Alex. Charlotte stood a few paces from him.

"My first warning came when the brakes on my car failed. I thought that it had been carelessness on my part, not maintaining the car properly until I took it to Calvin's Auto Shop and he found a tiny whole in the brake line, so small that it took days for the fluid to leak out. Calvin said that it had been deliberately made by someone. In fact Calvin was more concerned than I was and he had to convince me.

Francesca's eyes were fixed on this man whom she loved, and her mind was running back and forth between the names of Bud and Keal.

"And then when I started to lose all of my energy and felt just plain lousy, a friend suggested that I go to Dr. Samuel Grant, who is a nutritionist as well as a medical doctor. He took blood samples and samples of my hair, made test, and found that I was loaded with arsenic, and I didn't have the faintest idea where I was picking it up. So in order to save my life, I played dead. I took the *Sea Song* out, set her adrift, and took a rubber dinghy that I had brought aboard, so that I could leave the boat's dinghy on board, and rowed ashore.'' Everyone's eyes were glued to Keal as he spoke.

"What did you do for money, dear?'' Daisy asked. Keal smiled at her. "At first I had some cash, but later on a friend, Tom Lacy, who had worked on the docks before he opened his tavern, got me on there as a temporary worker.'' Keal laughed. "I got used to hard work.'' He spread his calloused hands out to show them what the heavy work had done to his hands.

"Oh, darling,'' Daisy gasped as she looked at the work-worn hands.

Keal was somber. "I don't regret it, Daisy.''

Ophelia listened intently. She had replaced the tiny pistol back into her purse now that the Chief had arrived. He still did not know what was going on.

Fergus's gaze, through his silver-rimmed glasses, never left Keal's face. He, too, was trying to understand what was happening. He finally asked, "I don't know what's going on here, Keal.''

"I must say at first I suspected you, Fergus. You were the most likely, I thought, not wanting to turn English Shipping over to me. After all, you did a darn good job of running the company and made it grow into what it is today.'' Keal looked at Fergus with kindness. "I want to thank you, Fergus.''

Amelia's voice was heard calling from downstairs. "Hello. Where is everyone?''

Francesca went to the head of the stairs and called down. "We're in the attic, Amelia."

Amelia came up the steps. "Why on earth is everyone in the attic, and what is the Chief's car doing out front?"

Francesca looked Amelia in the eyes and said, "You have a surprise coming, so steady yourself."

"Why! What is it?" Amelia pushed past Francesca with alarm. She stopped dead in her tracks and almost screamed. "Keal!" She rushed into his arms. "Oh, you bad boy. Where have you been?"

Francesca eased up to Keal and Amelia and said softly in her ear, "I want you to meet Bud."

Amelia drew back and looked from Keal to Francesca, and broke into laughter and said, "No!" Wiping her eyes, she suddenly realized that something serious was going on with the group that was gathered in the attic for some strange reason.

"Why is everyone up here?" she asked, becoming serious.

"Bu . . . Keal is telling us why he disappeared," Francesca said. "I'll fill you in later."

"All right," she agreed. "Finish, Keal," Amelia said with interest.

Charlotte turned to Fergus and spoke through bitter lips. "You fool, you worked your head off for this company and now you're going to step down and let a young sprig come in and take over, simply because someone in his family owned it over a hundred years ago. You did the work; you made English Shipping one of the largest tanker and freighter lines in the world. It should have been ours."

"You hit the key word, Charlotte. His family owned English Shipping and his aunt trusted me to look after it until he came of age." He looked sadly at Charlotte. "And that's what I have done, as a trusted friend." He rubbed his hands together. "And I might add, have become quite a rich man while doing so."

"Peanuts!" Charlotte spat out the word while Daisy and Lelia viewed their childhood friend in disbelief.

Keal placed a heavy-booted foot on an old box and thrust his hands into his pockets. He drew in a deep breath and his nostrils flared in anger as he gazed at Charlotte with contempt, and she returned his stare with a haughty arrogant stance. Keal suddenly pointed an accusing finger at her in rage.

"You let greed betray a long and trusted friendship. There is no excuse for such behavior. You tried to kill Daisy and Lelia!"

Fergus, who had found a dusty chair to sit on, rose quickly. "See here, Keal! This has gone far enough, and what exactly are you talking about?" He spoke in outrage to Keal.

"Let me explain it to you," Keal said patiently.

Francesca suddenly remembered the Rembrandt painting and went to the corner of the room where it lay spread out in the dim light. She picked it up and brought it out for everyone to see. "Could it have been for this?" Lelia and Daisy regarded the painting with just a small interest. "I don't think so," Lelia said softly.

"But it is very valuable."

"Yes, Francesca, but not worth anything compared to what is really at stake here." Lelia played with the edge of her dressing gown. She heaved a deep sigh. "Hardly a drop in the bucket, my dear." Keal's steady gaze fell on Lelia now. "I know what it is." A tear glistened in Lelia's eyes and she looked down at her old hands that were lined with blue veins and wrinkles.

More footsteps were heard coming up the steps. This time it was Dr. Defoe.

"Hello, everyone." He carried a brown paper sack in his hand. He reached inside it and brought out the crock that Charlotte often brought Sally's nourishing broth in.

At the sight of it, Charlotte drew back and the very quiet Axel said, "You stupid old fool!"

Fergus jumped to his feet again in outrage. "See here, Axel!" Fegus took a handkerchief from his breast pocket and wiped his wet brow. "This is preposterous."

"No, Fergus," Keal said.

"Will someone please tell me what is going on here?" Fergus rasped with a plea.

Keal took the crock from Dr. Defoe. He studied it for a moment.

"That's the culprit, all right," he said to Keal. At this moment, the chief remembered who he was and that he had not been invited as a spectator. He was the law, even if he didn't understand what the heck was going on. As far as he could see he wasn't the only one in the dark. Fergus Moore was in the same pit with him, so he didn't feel the complete fool that he had thought himself a moment ago. He boldly took the crock from Keal and asked, after examining it, "What the—excuse me, ladies." He nodded to the women apologetically. "What's going on here, English?"

"We're getting to it, Chief," Keal said.

"Okay," Congers said, pacified for the moment. Keal took the crock back.

"This is the reason Daisy and Lelia were becoming sick, and no one could figure out where the poison was coming from. I once read of a small boy becoming desperately sick and no one could figure out what was causing the listlessness, the pallor, and the dark circles that appeared under the child's eyes, so they finally put him into the hospital. They tested him for leukemia and found no signs of the disease. He began to improve almost at once, his color became normal again, and the kid was released from the hospital." Keal took in the people around him that were hanging on to his every word.

His eyes fell on Francesca and for a moment a warm sense of love moved in his cornflower-blue eyes as they lingered on her. Francesca lowered her eyes and blushed. A smile so small that no one noticed touched Keal's lips. He allowed his gaze to drift away from Francesca, who had difficulty regaining her composure. Amelia stole a glance at Francesca, and disregarding the seriousness of the situation, a twinkle lighted her eyes.

Keal continued. "But the kid went home and in no time the dark circles were back. He was listless again and no one could understand why it was just the boy. The doctor asked what did the boy use that no one else used in the house. His parents searched throughout the house and were virtually in a state of panic, when it dawned on them that he always drank his orange juice from a mug that they had bought in Mexico. They had it examined and found that the mug, when put into the kiln, had not been fired high enough. It seems that glazes are highly poisonous and unless fired at a very high temperature, cannot be used for eating or drinking, just for decorative purposes.

"It occurred to me one night as I lay in my room staring at the ceiling that Charlotte always brought me soup in a crock. This one." He held the crock up. "But I might add not before Francesca told me that her aunts were sick and that's when I had to call and tell you to get them to the hospital. I was glad that you answered, Francesca, because if Amelia had answered the phone, she would have known that it was me, but I had to take the chance, I would have had to let everyone know that I was still around and I didn't have the proof that I needed."

Daisy and Lelia were clearly uncomfortable and neither hardly raised their eyes from the surface of their dressing gowns.

"I got in touch with Ophelia. I asked her to go to Charlotte's, when she was not home, and make up a story to Sally about wanting to match a crock with Charlotte's so that she could give it to her as a gift. Of course, Sally let her borrow it."

Charlotte sucked in a breath. "Well, she can very well look for another position."

"You have a point there," Keal said dryly.

"Following through on my theory, Robert took the crock to Amanda Slade, who used to have a ceramic workshop. But after the death of her son, she gave it up because she feared that he had somehow gotten into the glazes. And the word from Amanda is the ware was fired too low to be used for foods of any kind." Keal turned again to Charlotte. "You knew this because you took ceramics classes with Amanda. I could understand why you might want to get rid of me, but I couldn't figure out why Lelia and Daisy." Keal addressed Daisy and Lelia. "You of course did not suspect anything like this. But you all held a secret. I had no idea of this, and I suppose I wasn't to know until Amelia's twenty-fifth birthday." Amelia looked surprised. "I remember Aunt Isabel telling me one day, patting her night table, she said, 'This is my secret hiding place.' So after much too long, it occurred to me that whatever was behind all of this might just be there. I pulled all the drawers out and found nothing. I leaned it over to look behind it, and a little drawer slipped out. Upright it looked just like a molding over the drawer. When the compartment pushed out I found this envelope containing two documents." Keal paused for a moment, slapping the envelope against his hand. He said, "One was a birth certificate and the other a certificate of death."

Chapter Fifteen

Keal's eyes sought Daisy's and Lelia's. Tears
streamed down Lelia's cheeks as she raised her eyes
to meet Keal's and he said, "No one on earth has
ever been better friends then Lelia and Daisy and I
think Aunt Isabel thought that she could have said
the same about Charlotte. But you can't always tell
about these things."

Francesca rushed to Lelia and cradled her against
her chest. "Don't cry, Aunt Lelia, everything will
be all right."

Lelia caressed her hand and said, "It's all right,
dear. It's all right." She gently removed Francesca's
arms from around her shoulders and stood up. She
wiped her eyes and her body became regal once
again.

"Charlotte, I must admit that after all these years
you had me fooled. I thought that you had loved
Isabel as much as Daisy and me, that our friendship
had been more than special. We could have all been
sisters and if ever any one of us needed the other,

there was no question that all would have been there.'' Lelia's eyes narrowed in anger as she looked at Charlotte, who would not meet Lelia's accusatory glare. ''But all the time you were jealous of Isabel and you betrayed all of us, but most of all, Charlotte, you betrayed yourself because you cut yourself from our bond, which will always be more valuable then mere money. You forget, Charlotte, that money does not have a soul.''

She turned to Keal. ''It was not to be done this way, but circumstances have necessitated this radical change. Humph,'' Lelia said under her breath with a slight shake of her head in disbelief.

She turned her eyes to Keal and said, ''Sit down, Keal. Francesca has given me a very important letter from Hadley's.'' She noticed Keal take Francesca's hand in his; with a dry smile she quipped, ''This family is full of secrets.'' Lelia spoke as if she were making an address at a ladies' luncheon. She reached into the pocket of her dressing gown and took out her spectacles. She tore the end of the letter open and read it to herself for a moment, then she looked at the waiting faces that stared at her.

She began, ''The death certificate is that of Clarissa Lynche, Isabel's daughter.'' Lelia swallowed hard. ''Clarissa did not die in an automobile accident.'' This time Lelia drew in a breath with a shudder. ''Clarissa died in childbirth.''

A gasp went through the room. Charlotte's eyes remained glued to the floor. Lelia then turned to Amelia and with warm and caring eyes she said, ''Amelia, you were Clarissa's child.''

Amelia went pale and she started to tremble. Francesca hurried to Amelia and put her arms around her. Daisy lifted her weighty body and went to cradle Amelia in her arms.

"I want you to know, darling, that your grandmother loved you very much. From the moment she heard of your existence, she made arrangements for you to be cared for. Times have changed and in some respects for the better, but she was trying to protect Clarissa from scandal. You can understand that, can't you, dear? The morals of today are very new to us. But whatever morality was in our day, it never had any bearing on our love for you. We've waited to tell you when we thought you were old enough to understand." Daisy smiled at Amelia and stroked her hair. "We thought twenty-five a good age. I know that your birthday isn't until next month, but what's a few weeks?" Amelia managed a weak smile at Daisy's attempt to be amusing.

Keal walked over to Amelia and squatted down before her. "Hi, cuz." A little laugh emitted from Amelia mixed with a sob, and she said to Keal with a shy spread of her hands, "Hi, cuz." He clasped both of her hands, "We're not a bad family, you know." This time she laughed out loud.

Lelia spoke again. "We know what the ransacking of the house was for. You were looking for Amelia's birth certificate. If we were out of the way there would be no evidence of Amelia's birth and her right to share part of the English Shipping fortune." Lelia held up the papers from Hadley's. "This is the will that Isabel made a few years before she died. You remember visiting Isabel quite often, don't you, Amelia?''

''Why, yes,'' Amelia answered.

''That was so that your grandmother would know and love you.''

Keal got up and went to Lelia's side. He put his arms around her shoulders.

''With me out of the way and all evidence of Amelia destroyed, there would be nothing to keep the English company from going completely into the hands of Axel. Once Fergus retired and with no other family members to bother with, the company would have been virtually his and Charlotte's. Poor Fergus, you knew nothing of this. If you had, you would have put a stop to it and canned Axel.''

Fergus took his glasses off and wiped them vigorously and said with controlled anger, ''I certainly would have, Axel, and you would never have had another job, not even that of a janitor.''

Axel made no reply, and Fergus continued contemptuously, ''But I suppose you will be mopping up a lot of hallways where you're headed.'' He put his glasses on again with a disheartened effort. He knew that Charlotte would have to be prosecuted along with Axel.

The room became deathly quiet with each pondering their own thoughts. Charlotte in a sudden fit of irritation decided to depart.

''I have had enough of this nonsense and I will not stay here another minute and listen to these ridiculous accusations.'' She turned to go down the steps, and Chief Congers called out to her.

"Hold on there, Mrs. Moore." He reached to grab her arm. She glared at him with disdain and whipped her arm from his grasp and for one desperate moment she teetered on the rounded edge of the landing. The fine smooth leather of the sole of her shoes slipped and she tumbled down to the bottom of the stairs as frantic hands tried to save her. Screams echoed through the room as the sound of scuffling feet rushed to Charlotte's aid but they were not heard by her. Chief Congers reached her first where she lay sprawled halfway across the steps at the bottom landing with her neck twisted in an odd way.

Fergus bent over Charlotte, tears running down his cheeks through the silver rim of his glasses as he gently touched her pale face. The chief looked at Fergus with regret. "I think her neck is broken."

Dr. Defoe pushed the chief aside and knelt down beside Charlotte's still figure. He touched her head gently and felt gingerly for any hint of a pulse. He stood up and told Congers to call for an ambulance, then beckoned to Keal to take the women away. Keal put his arms around Lelia and Daisy and helped them pass Charlotte.

Francesca, Amelia, and Ophelia followed to the drawing room where Daisy sat heavily on the divan and Ophelia sat down with her. Francesca sat next to Lelia, while a deeply thoughtful Amelia stood before the fireplace.

The wail of the ambulance siren pierced the air and died down with a whine as the vehicle came to a stop. Keal went to the door and showed the attendants the way up to the attic.

Lelia sat very erect on the sofa, her white hair locked in place by the black velvet ribbon, while Daisy sat wiping away tears that would not stop falling.

Lelia touched Francesca's hand and said, "Tell Ruth to bring in some tea and brandy. We need something to help us get through this day."

Francesca left the room, glad for something to do, but, when she opened the door and heard the distant voices in the attic, she ran into the kitchen and shut the door tightly behind her, the horror of the day was just becoming real to her.

The medical examiner had come and they were allowed to remove Charlotte's body, and the chief left with Axel.

Dr. Defoe and Keal left with Fergus to take care of the necessary arrangements. Ophelia stayed behind with the Gaylord family as support. They all remained seated in the same place. No one felt the strength to move. Francesca finally asked her aunts why they had kept a Rembrandt in the attic.

"Well, dear . . ." Daisy turned her gaze to Amelia. "When you were born you can imagine the state of confusion that reigned here. Your mother was dead, the barriers of secrecy that had to be built and maintained, and then there was you." Love swam in Daisy's eyes. "A beautiful little thing who also had to be looked after. The woman who delivered you looked after you for a few days until after your mother's funeral. Then Lelia and I went to Hornsville. We found a competent woman to care for you and she also grew to love you and wanted to adopt

you.'' Daisy smiled. ''You were never without love.
After that we went to New York and purchased the
Rembrandt, which we knew would never decrease
in value. Fergus had a broker transfer the money to
Lelia and me for the painting. This was to be your
legacy. But as the years went by and your grandmother grew to love you with all her heart, she had
Hadley's in Philadelphia draw up another will, with
you inheriting Clarissa's half of English Shipping.
That's what Charlotte was trying to keep from coming to light.''

Amelia looked at Francesca as if a light had just
come on in her head. ''Do you know, Francesca, I'll
bet that was Charlotte in the house. You remember—
she had changed the day from Tuesday to Wednesday because she knew that you had a class, and
everyone would be out of the house, and that's why
she was late.''

''Of course,'' Francesca said, sounding vindi-
cated. ''And Charlotte has always had a key.''

''I will never understand Charlotte,'' Daisy said.

The shrill ring of the telephone startled all of
them. Ophelia was the only one who made a move
to answer it.

''Oh, hello, Keal.'' She listened intently. ''Oh,
no.'' All eyes turned to Ophelia, then they heard her
say, ''It's for the best, and a blessing for Fergus, it's
over. Yes, I'll ask.'' She cupped her hand over the
mouth of the phone.

''Keal wants you to spend the night at Belle Rose.
I think it's a good idea.''

''So do I. We'll take Ruth with us. Tell him yes,''

Lelia said. They heard Ophelia say, "Yes, yes I will. Keal has asked me to stay with you at Belle Rose tonight."

"You're a good friend, Ophelia," Daisy said.

"I'm a good friend, Daisy," Ophelia said with irony in her voice. "Ladies, let me put an end to my being a relative of Mrs. Hyde. She and I don't know each other from Adam. Daisy was visiting her, but she found me sitting on a park bench crying my heart out. I'd lost my job, and lost the room that I was renting. All of my belongings sat beside me on the ground. Daisy stopped, sat down beside me, and asked if she could help me. I of course poured my woes out to her." Ophelia fought back a sob. "And this lady said come back to Edgecombe with me, I have a house big enough to house an army. Robert needed someone in his office. She recommended me. And as the saying goes the rest is history. I owe my life to her."

"Well, Ophelia," Daisy said, "let's say it was a lucky day for both of us."

"I've also been putting off some more unpleasant news with my story." Ophelia sat down again. "Keal just told me that Chief Congers paid Axel the courtesy of letting him pick up a few personal things from home, and Axel went to his bedroom and shot himself to death." There was a huge gasp from the four women. "Keal said this saves Fergus any more suffering. The chief has written up Charlotte's death as accidental, which it was, and Axel's as 'death by his own hands, reasons unknown.' The chief said you can't put two dead people on trial."

"That's as good a reason as any," Lelia said sadly.

The doorbell rang, and there was a happier-looking Cyrus waiting with the blue limousine. Francesca was quite surprised.

Keal met them at the door at Belle Rose, looking quite different from the Bud that Francesca had known. Elegant and richly dressed, he welcomed all of them with a kiss to the cheek.

"Dinner will be ready soon." When they were in the doorway, he spoke to Amelia. "You will want to wait for Bill, I suppose, so I'm leaving the keys to Lyre Hall here on the table. You and Bill might want to look at it together. It's yours, you know. Bill was an awful lot of help to me, taking time off from work to do the things that I couldn't do. I don't think I can ever repay him, nor Tom Lacy."

"Keal." Amelia looked at him with uncertainty in her eyes. "Do you think that I will ever get used to all this?"

He laughed and kissed her on the forehead "Amelia, I don't think you will have any problem."

They entered the sitting room. "Ladies, I'm going to borrow Francesca for a while." He took her by the hand and led her back into the entrance hall. "I have your Christmas present." He took a black velvet case from the table, and opened it, where the most exquisite diamond necklace of floral sprays lay. "I'm reminding you of my promise," he said, and took another black velvet box from his pocket. He opened it and Francesca saw the most beautiful emerald-cut diamond ring. Keal put it gently on her left-hand ring finger. ''And this is to let everyone know that you belong to me.''

''Oh, darling.'' Francesca was so overcome that she put her head on Keal's chest and wept, with his arms firmly enfolding her.

''Now, I think it's time I took you aboard the *Sea Song*.''

Daisy and Lelia watched Francesca and Keal walking along the beach.

''Do you smell Chanel Number 5?''

''You know, I believe I do,'' Daisy said, smiling with satisfaction. Everything had worked out fine.